"Have you always lived in New York, Dick?" asked Frank, after a pause.

"Ever since I can remember."

"Have you got any father or mother?"

"I ain't got no mother. She died when I was three years old. My father went to sea; but he went off before mother died, and nothin' was ever heard of him. I expect he got wrecked, or died at sea."

"And what happened to you when your mother died?"

"The folks she boarded with took care of me, but they was poor, and they couldn't do much. When I was seven, the woman died, and her husband went out West, and then I had to scratch for myself."

"At seven years old!" exclaimed Frank, in amazement.

A Background Note about *Ragged Dick*

Ragged Dick is set in New York City in the 1860s. Then, as now, there were wealthy people and fancy stores in the city. And then, as now, there were thousands of people living in poverty.

There were no subways. Instead of motorized buses, there were horse-drawn omnibuses or horse-cars. Instead of trucks, there were horse-drawn wagons. Instead of cars, there were carriages.

At that time, many poor boys earned money by selling newspapers or shining men's shoes. The boys who polished shoes were called bootblacks.

In the 1860s, each piece of paper money had the name of a specific bank printed on it. And the value of money was very different. Ten dollars a week was a very large salary for a young clerk working in an office. One could get a meal in a restaurant for twenty-five cents or ride the ferry to Brooklyn for two cents. A man's suit, a couple of shirts, a pair of shoes, and a cap could be purchased for about twenty dollars.

This is the world that Ragged Dick, a fourteen-year-old homeless boy, lives in.

HORATIO ALGER, JR.

RAGGED DICK OR STREET LIFE IN NEW YORK

Edited, and with an Afterword,
by Bill Blauvelt

 THE TOWNSEND LIBRARY

RAGGED DICK
OR STREET LIFE IN NEW YORK

TP THE TOWNSEND LIBRARY

For more titles in the Townsend Library,
visit our website: **www.townsendpress.com**

Townsend Press, Inc.
439 Kelley Drive
West Berlin, New Jersey 08091

ISBN-13: 978-1-59194-080-7
ISBN-10: 1-59194-080-X

Library of Congress Control Number:
2006934268

CONTENTS

CHAPTER 1

Ragged Dick Is Introduced to the Reader

"Wake up there, youngster," said a rough voice.

Ragged Dick opened his eyes slowly. He stared blankly in the face of the speaker but did not move to get up.

"Wake up, you young loafer!" said the man a little impatiently. "I suppose you'd lay there all day, if I hadn't called you."

"What time is it?" asked Dick.

"Seven o'clock."

"Seven o'clock! I oughter have been up an hour ago. I went to the show at the Old Bowery last night, and didn't turn in till past twelve. No wonder I overslept."

"You went to the Old Bowery? Where'd you get your money?" asked the man. He was a messenger who worked for a business on Spruce Street.

"Made it shining shoes, of course. My guardian don't allow me no money for theaters, so I have to earn it," he added with a grin.

"Some boys get it easier than that," said the messenger significantly.

"You don't catch me stealin', if that's what you mean," said Dick.

"Don't you ever steal, then?"

"No, and I wouldn't. Lots of boys does it, but I wouldn't."

"Well, I'm glad to hear you say that. I believe there's some good in you, Dick, after all."

"Oh, I'm a rough customer!" said Dick. "But I wouldn't steal. It's mean."

"I'm glad you think so, Dick." The rough voice sounded gentler than at first. "Have you got any money to buy your breakfast?"

"No, but I'll soon get some."

While this conversation had been going on, Dick had gotten up. His bedroom had been a wooden box half-full of straw. The young boot-black had slept in his clothes.

He jumped out of the box, shook himself, and picked out one or two straws that had found their way into tears in his clothes. Pulling his well-worn cap over his uncombed hair, he was all ready for the business of the day.

Dick's appearance as he stood beside the box was rather peculiar. His pants were torn in several places. They had apparently once belonged to a boy two sizes larger than he was. His vest had only two buttons. Out of it peeked a shirt that looked as if it had been worn for a month. To complete his costume he wore a ragged coat that was too long for him.

Dick was above such refinements as washing his hands and face. He had no particular dislike of dirt and did not think it necessary to remove several dark streaks on his face and hands. But in spite of his dirt and rags, there was something about him that caught people's attention. He had a frank, straightforward manner that made him appealing. He had a surprising maturity for a fourteen year old.

Dick's business hours had commenced. He had no office to open. His shoeshine box was ready for use, and he looked sharply in the faces of all who passed, asking each, "Shine yer boots, sir?"

"How much?" asked a gentleman on his way to his office.

"Ten cents," said Dick, sinking to his knees on the sidewalk, flourishing his brush with the air of one skilled in his profession.

"Ten cents! Isn't that a little steep?"

"Well, you know 'taint all clear profit," Dick said, setting to work. "There's the polish costs something, and I have to get a new brush pretty often."

"And you have a large rent too, I imagine," the gentleman joked, as he looked at a large tear in Dick's coat.

"Yes, sir," said Dick, always ready to joke. "I have to pay such a big rent for my mansion up on Fifth Avenue that I can't afford to take less than ten cents a shine. I'll give you a bully shine, sir."

"Be quick about it. I am in a hurry. So your house is on Fifth Avenue, is it?"

"It isn't anywhere else," grinned Dick, for he spoke the truth there.

"Who is your tailor?" asked the gentleman, looking over Dick's clothing.

"Would you like to go to the same one?" asked Dick.

"Well, no. It strikes me that he didn't give you a very good fit."

"This coat once belonged to General Washington," said Dick, comically. "He wore it all through the Revolution, and it got torn some, 'cause he fought so hard. When he died he told his widow to give it to some smart young feller that hadn't got no coat of his own. So she gave it to me. But if you'd like it, sir, to remember General Washington by, I'll let you have it reasonable."

"Thank you, but I wouldn't want to deprive you of it. It seems you have distinguished friends. Now, my lad, I suppose you would like your money."

"I don't have any objection," said Dick.

"I believe," said the gentleman, examining his change, "I haven't got anything smaller than twenty-five cents. Have you got any change?"

"Not a cent," said Dick. "All my money's invested in the Erie Railroad."

"That's unfortunate."

"Shall I get the money changed, sir?"

"I can't wait; I've got an appointment. I'll give you a quarter, and you can leave the change at my office any time during the day."

"All right, sir. Where is it?"

"125 Fulton Street. Will you remember?"

"Yes, sir. What name?"

"Greyson. The office is on the second floor."

"All right, sir. I'll bring it."

"I wonder whether the little scamp will prove honest," said Mr. Greyson to himself, as he walked away. "If he does, I'll give him my business regularly."

Mr. Greyson didn't understand Dick. He wasn't a model boy in all respects. He swore sometimes, and now and then he played tricks upon boys from the country, or gave a wrong direction to honest old gentlemen unused to the city.

Another of Dick's faults was his extravagance. Because he was always on the lookout for business, he earned enough to have supported himself comfortably and respectably. But Dick was careless with his earnings. However much he managed to earn during the day, all was generally spent before the next morning. He liked going to the Old Bowery Theater. If he had any money left afterward, he would invite some of his friends in somewhere to have an oyster stew.

There was another way in which Dick sometimes lost money. There was a noted gambling-house on Baxter Street. In the evening it was sometimes crowded with boys like Dick. They bet their hard earned money, generally losing of course, and refreshed themselves from time to time with a vile mixture of liquor at two cents a glass. Sometimes Dick strayed in there and spent the evening gambling.

But there were some good points about Dick in spite of his faults. He was above doing anything mean or dishonorable. He would not steal, or cheat, or bully younger boys. He was frank and straightforward, resourceful and self-reliant. His nature was a noble one.

CHAPTER 2

Johnny Nolan

After Dick had finished polishing Mr. Greyson's boots he was fortunate enough to get three other customers.

When Dick finished with his last customer, the City Hall clock struck eight o'clock. He had been up an hour and hard at work. Now he began to think about breakfast. He walked down Nassau Street until he reached Ann Street. On this street was a small, cheap restaurant where for five cents Dick could get a cup of coffee. For ten cents more he could get a plate of beefsteak with a piece of bread thrown in. These Dick ordered. Then he sat down at one of the plain tables.

Dick had scarcely been served when he saw a boy about his own size standing at the door looking hungrily into the restaurant. It was Johnny Nolan, a boy of fourteen. Like Ragged Dick, he was a bootblack.

"Had your breakfast, Johnny?" asked Dick, cutting off a piece of steak.

"No."

"Come in, then. Here's room for you."

"I ain't got no money," said Johnny, looking a little enviously at his friend.

"Haven't you had any shines?"

"Yes, I had one, but I won't get paid till to-morrow."

"Are you hungry?"

"Try me, and see."

"Come in. I'll treat you this morning."

Johnny Nolan quickly accepted this invitation and sat down beside Dick.

"What'll you have, Johnny?"

"Same as you."

"Cup o' coffee and beefsteak," ordered Dick.

When these were brought, Johnny attacked them vigorously.

In the bootblacking business, as in other jobs, energy and hard work are rewarded, and laziness is not. Dick was energetic and on the alert for business, but Johnny was not. The result was that Dick earned probably three times as much as his friend.

"How do you like it?" asked Dick, surveying Johnny's attacks upon the steak with pleasure.

"It's hunky."

"Do you come here often?" asked Johnny.

"Most every day. You ought to come too."

"I can't afford it."

"What do you do with your money?" asked Dick.

"I don't get near as much as you, Dick."

"Well you might if you tried. I keep my eyes open—that's the way I get jobs. You're lazy, that's what's the matter."

Johnny felt the truth of this remark. He said nothing and continued eating the breakfast.

Breakfast over, Dick walked up to the desk and settled the bill. Then, followed by Johnny, he went out into the street.

"Where are you going, Johnny?"

"Up to Mr. Taylor's, on Spruce Street, to see if he don't want a shine."

"Do you work for him regular?"

"Yes. Him and his partner wants a shine most every day. Where are you goin'?"

"Down front of the Astor House Hotel. I guess I'll find some customers there."

At this moment Johnny dodged into an entryway and hid behind the door, to Dick's surprise.

"What's the matter now?" asked Dick.

"Has he gone?" asked Johnny, anxiously.

"Has who gone?"

"That man in the brown coat."

"What of him. You ain't scared of him, are you?"

"Yes, he got me a place to work once."

"Where?"

"Ever so far off."

"What if he did?"

"I ran away."

"Didn't you like it?"

"No, I had to get up too early. It was on a farm, and I had to get up at five to take care of the cows. I like New York best."

"Didn't they give you enough to eat?"

"Oh, yes, plenty."

"And you had a good bed?"

"Yes."

"Then you'd better have stayed. You don't get either of them here. Where'd you sleep last night?"

"Up an alley in an old wagon."

"You had a better bed than that in the country, didn't you?"

"Yes, it was as soft as—as cotton."

"Why didn't you stay?"

"I felt lonely," said Johnny.

Johnny had but one tie to bind him to the city. He had a father living, but he might as well have been without one. Mr. Nolan was a drunkard and spent most of his money on liquor. He was never a very gentle man, but drink made him truly ugly. Sometimes he would get into such a rage that Johnny's life was in danger. Some months before, he had thrown an iron skillet at his son's head with such terrific force that it would have killed Johnny if he had not ducked in time. The boy ran from the house and had not dared return. Somebody had given him a brush and box of polish, and he had set up in business for himself.

"How'd you get away?" asked Dick, with some curiosity. "Did you walk?"

"No, I rode on the railroad cars."

"Where'd you get your money?"

"I didn't have none."

"What did you do, then?"

"I got up about three o'clock and walked to Albany."

"Where's that?" asked Dick, whose ideas of geography were rather vague.

"Up the river."

"How far?"

"About a thousand miles," said Johnny, whose concept of distance was equally vague.

"What did you do then?"

"I hid on top of a freight car and came all the way without their seeing me. That man in the brown coat was the man that got me the place, and I'm afraid he'd want to send me back."

"Well," said Dick, reflectively, "I dunno as I'd like to live in the country. I couldn't go to the Old Bowery or Baxter Street. There wouldn't be no place to spend my evenings. But it's tough in winter, Johnny, 'specially when your overcoat's at the tailor's, an' likely to stay there."

"That's true, Dick. But I gotta get goin', or Mr. Taylor'll get somebody else to shine his boots."

Johnny walked back to Nassau Street, while Dick kept on his way to Broadway.

"That boy," Dick said to himself, "ain't got no ambition. I'll bet he won't get five shines today. I'm glad I ain't like him. I couldn't go to the theater nor get half as much as I wanted to eat. — Shine yer boots, sir?"

This remark was addressed to a stylishly

dressed young man.

"I've had my boots polished once already this morning, but this confounded mud has spoiled the shine."

"I'll make 'em all right, sir, in a minute."

"Go ahead, then."

The boots were soon polished in Dick's best style.

"I haven't got any change," said the young man, fumbling in his pocket, "but here's a bill you may run somewhere and get changed. I'll pay you five cents extra for your trouble."

He produced a five-dollar bill, which Dick took into a store close by.

"Will you please change that, sir?" said Dick, walking up to the counter.

The salesman took the bill, and, slightly glancing at it, exclaimed angrily, "Be off, you young loafer, or I'll have you arrested."

"What's wrong?"

"You've offered me a counterfeit bill."

"I didn't know it," said Dick.

"Don't tell me. Be off, or I'll have you arrested."

CHAPTER 3

Dick Makes a Proposal

Though Dick was startled to discover that the five-dollar bill he was counterfeit, he stood his ground bravely.

"Clear out of this shop, you young loafer," repeated the clerk.

"Then give me back my bill."

"So you can try to cheat someone else? No, sir, I'll do no such thing."

"It doesn't belong to me," said Dick. "A gentleman that owes me for a shine gave it to me to change."

"A likely story," said the clerk, but he seemed a little uneasy.

"I'll go and call him," said Dick.

He went out and found his customer standing on the Astor House steps.

"Well, youngster, have you brought back my change? You took a long time about it. I began to think you had taken off with the money."

"That ain't my style," said Dick, proudly.

"Then where's the change?"

"I haven't got it."

"Where's the bill then?"

"I haven't got that either."

"You young rascal!"

"Hold on a minute, mister," said Dick, "and I'll tell you all about it. The man what took the bill said it wasn't good and kept it."

"The bill was perfectly good. So he kept it, did he? We'll see if he won't give it back to me!"

Dick led the way, and the gentleman followed him into the store. At the reappearance of Dick with the well-dressed man, the clerk looked nervous. He knew that he could browbeat a ragged bootblack, but with a gentleman he saw that it would be a different matter. He pretended to be busy replacing goods on the shelves.

"Now," said the young man, "point out the clerk that has my money."

"That's him," said Dick, pointing to the clerk.

The gentleman walked up to the counter.

"I will trouble you," he said, "for the five-dollar bill which that boy offered you, and which you still have."

"It was a bad bill," said the clerk, his cheeks turning red and his manner nervous.

"It was not. We will look at it together and decide the matter."

The clerk fumbled in his vest-pocket and drew out a counterfeit bill.

"This is a bad bill, but it is not the one I gave the boy."

"It is the one he gave me."

The young man looked doubtful.

"Boy," he said to Dick, "is this the bill you gave to this man?"

"No, it isn't."

"You lie, you young rascal!" exclaimed the

clerk. He was beginning to find himself in a tight place and could not see the way out.

The scene attracted the attention of everyone in the store, and the owner walked up from the far end, where he had been busy.

"What's all this, Mr. Hatch?" he demanded.

"That boy," said the clerk, "came in and asked change for a bad bill. I kept the bill and told him to clear out. Now he wants it again to pass on somebody else."

"Show the bill."

The merchant looked at it. "Yes, that's a bad bill," he said. "There is no doubt about that."

"But it is not the one the boy offered," said Dick's patron. "It is a five-dollar bill, but on a different bank."

"Do you remember what bank it was on?"

"It was on the Merchants' Bank of Boston."

"Are you sure of it?"

"I am."

"Perhaps the boy kept it and offered the other."

"You may search me if you want to," said Dick, indignantly.

"He doesn't look as if he was likely to have any extra bills. I suspect that your clerk pocketed the good bill and has substituted the counterfeit one. It is a nice little scheme of his for making money "

"I haven't seen any bill on the Merchants'

Bank," said the clerk, doggedly.

"You had better feel in your pockets."

"This matter must be resolved," said the merchant, firmly. "If you have the bill, produce it."

"I haven't got it," said the clerk. But he looked guilty nonetheless.

"I demand that he be searched," said Dick's patron.

"I tell you I haven't got it."

"Shall I send for a police officer, Mr. Hatch, or will you allow yourself to be searched quietly?" said the merchant.

Alarmed at the threat implied in these words, the clerk put his hand into his vest pocket, and drew out a five-dollar bill on the Merchants' Bank.

"Is this your note?" asked the shopkeeper, showing it to the young man.

"It is."

"I must have made a mistake," faltered the clerk.

"You will not have a chance to make another mistake in my store," the merchant said sternly. "You may go up to the office and collect what wages are due you. I have no further need for your services."

As the clerk walked glumly toward the back of the store, the well-dressed young man got change for his five-dollar bill.

"Now, youngster," he said to Dick as they went out of the store, "I must pay you something extra for your trouble. Here's fifty cents."

"Thank you, sir," said Dick. "You're very kind. Don't you want some more bills changed?"

"Not today," said he with a smile. "It's too expensive."

Dick shouldered his box and walked up as far as the Astor House Hotel. He took his station on the sidewalk and began to look about him.

Just behind him were two people—a gentleman of fifty and a boy of thirteen or fourteen. They were speaking together, and Dick had no difficulty in hearing what they said.

"I am sorry, Frank, that I can't show you some of the sights of New York, but I have a very busy schedule today. This is your first visit to the city, too."

"Yes, sir."

"There's a good deal worth seeing here. But I'm afraid you'll have to wait to next time. You can go out and walk by yourself. But don't go too far, or you will get lost."

Frank looked disappointed.

"I wish Tom Miles knew I was here," he said. "He would show me around."

"Where does he live?"

"Somewhere up town, I believe."

"I'm afraid we do not have much chance of finding him. If you would rather go with me than stay here, you can. But I will be tied up in merchants' accounting offices, and I am afraid it would not be very interesting."

"I think," said Frank, after a little hesitation, "that I will go off by myself. I won't go very far. And if I lose my way, I will ask directions for the Astor House."

"Yes, anybody will direct you here. Very well, Frank, I am sorry I can't do better for you."

"Oh, never mind, uncle, I'll enjoy walking around and looking at the shop-windows."

Dick had listened to this conversation. Being an enterprising young man, he saw an opportunity and decided to take advantage of it.

He stepped up to the two just as Frank's uncle was about to leave and said, "I know all about the city, sir; I'll show him around, if you want me to."

The gentleman looked curiously at the ragged figure before him.

"So you are a city boy, are you?"

"Yes, sir," said Dick, "I've lived here ever since I was a baby."

"And you know all about the places of interest, I suppose?"

"Yes, sir."

"And Central Park?"

"Yes, sir. I know my way round."

The gentleman looked thoughtful.

"I don't know what to say, Frank," he

remarked after a while. "It is rather a novel proposal. He isn't exactly the sort of guide I would have picked out for you. Still he looks honest. He has an open face, and I think can be depended upon."

"I wish he wasn't so ragged and dirty," said Frank, who felt a little shy about being seen with such a companion.

"I'm afraid you haven't washed your face this morning," said the man.

"They didn't have no wash-bowls at the hotel where I stopped," said Dick.

"What hotel did you stop at?"

"The Box Hotel."

"The Box Hotel?"

"Yes, sir, I slept in a box on Spruce Street."

Frank surveyed Dick curiously.

"How did you like it?" he asked.

"I slept bully."

"What if it had rained?"

"Then I'd have got my best clothes wet," said Dick.

"Are these all the clothes you have?"

"Yes, sir."

The uncle spoke a few words to Frank, who seemed pleased with the suggestion.

"Follow me, my lad," he said.

Dick followed Frank and his uncle into the hotel, past the office, to the foot of the staircase. Here a clerk of the hotel stopped Dick.

"It's all right," Frank's uncle said. "This young man is with me."

"Oh, if he is with you, Mr. Whitney, then it is quite all right," said the clerk. Then, turning back to Dick, he said, "Excuse me. I didn't realize you were with Mr. Whitney."

They went up the stairs, entered a long hallway, and finally paused before a door. Mr. Whitney opened the door and they entered a pleasant room.

"Come in, my lad," said Mr. Whitney.

Dick and Frank entered.

CHAPTER 4

Dick's New Suit

"**N**ow," said Mr. Whitney to Dick, "my nephew here is on his way to a boarding school. He has a suit of clothes in his trunk about half worn. He is willing to give it to you. I think it will look better than the clothes you have on."

Dick hardly knew what to say. Presents were something that he knew very little about. He had never been given one before. To get so large a gift from a stranger seemed wonderful.

Frank then brought out a neat gray suit and a clean shirt.

"Before you put them on, my lad, you must wash yourself. Clean clothes and a dirty skin don't go very well together. Frank, show him where he can wash up. I must to go at once. Have you got enough money?"

"Yes, uncle."

"One more word, my lad," said Mr. Whitney, addressing Dick. "I may be rash in trusting a boy whom I know nothing about. But I like your looks, and I think you will prove a proper guide for my nephew."

"Yes, I will, sir," said Dick, earnestly. "I promise!"

"Very well. Have a good time."

Dick washed, and he found the sensation of cleanliness both new and pleasant. Frank added to his gift a pair of socks and an old pair of shoes. "I am sorry I haven't a cap for you," said he.

"I've got one," said Dick.

"It isn't so new as it might be," said Frank, looking at Dick's hat. It was dingy, with a large hole in the top and a piece of the rim torn off.

"No," said Dick; "my grandfather used to wear it when he was a boy, and I've kep' it ever since out of respect for his memory. But I'll get a new one now. I can buy one cheap on Chatham Street."

"Is that near here?"

"Only five minutes' walk."

"Then we can get one on the way."

When Dick was dressed in his new clothing, with his face clean and his hair brushed, it was difficult to imagine that he was the same boy.

He looked quite handsome. He might have been taken for a young gentleman, except that his hands were red and stained with shoe polish.

"Look at yourself," said Frank, pointing to the mirror.

"By gracious!" said Dick, starting back in astonishment. "That isn't me, is it?"

"Don't you know yourself?" asked Frank, smiling.

"What'll Johnny Nolan say when he sees me? He won't dare to speak to me. Ain't it rich?" And Dick burst into a loud laugh. Then he looked gratefully at Frank. "You're a brick," he said.

"A what?"

"A brick! You're a good fellow to give me such a present."

"You're quite welcome, Dick," said Frank, kindly. "I'm better off than you are, and I can spare the clothes just as well as not. Are you ready to go?"

"Wait a minute till I get my handkerchief," and Dick pulled a dirty rag from the pocket of his old pants.

"You mustn't carry that," said Frank.

"But I've got a cold," said Dick.

"Oh, I don't mean you to go without a handkerchief. I'll give you one."

Frank opened his suitcase and pulled out two, which he gave to Dick.

"I wonder if I ain't dreamin'" said Dick, once more looking at himself doubtfully in the mirror. "I'm afraid I'm dreamin' and will wake up in a barrel, as I did night afore last."

"Maybe you should pinch yourself to be sure you're awake," Frank said.

"May I'd better," said Dick. "But what should I do with my brush and polish?"

"You can leave them here till we come back," said Frank. "They will be safe."

"Hold on a minute," said Dick, looking at Frank's boots with a professional eye, "you ain't got a good shine on them boots. I'll make 'em shine so you can see your face in 'em."

And he was as good as his word.

"Thank you," said Frank; "now you had better brush your own shoes."

This had not occurred to Dick. In general the professional bootblack considers his polish too valuable to waste on his own shoes or boots.

The two boys went downstairs together. They met the same clerk who had spoken to Dick a few minutes before, but there was no sign of recognition.

"He don't know me," said Dick. "He thinks I'm a young swell like you."

"What's a swell?"

"Oh, a feller that wears fancy clothes like you."

"And you, too, Dick."

"Yes," said Dick, "who'd ever have thought I would turn into a swell?"

They left the Astor House Hotel and were walking along the west side by the park, when Dick spotted Johnny Nolan.

Dick could not wait to see Johnny's amazement at his change in appearance. He stole up behind him, and slapped him on the back.

"Hallo, Johnny, how many shines have you had?"

Johnny turned round expecting to see Dick, whose voice he recognized. But his astonished eyes rested on boy who looked like Dick but certainly wasn't dressed like him.

"What luck, Johnny?" repeated Dick.

Johnny looked him over from head to foot in great bewilderment.

"Who are you?" he said.

"Well, that's a good one," laughed Dick. "So you don't know Dick?"

"Where'd you get all them clothes?" asked Johnny. "Have you been stealin'?"

"Say that again, and I'll lick you. No, I've lent my clothes to a young feller as was goin' to a party and didn't have none good enough to wear. And I put on my second-best for a change."

Without any further explanation, Dick went off, followed by the astonished gaze of Johnny Nolan. Johnny could not quite make up his mind whether the neat-looking boy he had been talking with was really Ragged Dick or not.

In order to reach Chatham Street it was necessary to cross Broadway. This was easier said than done. There was such a crowd of omnibuses, wagons, carriages, and vehicles of all kinds that the crossing was a challenge to someone who is not used to it. Dick made nothing of it, dodging in and out among the horses and wagons with ease.

Reaching the opposite sidewalk, he looked back and found that Frank had retreated in dismay.

"Come across!" called out Dick.

"I don't see any chance," said Frank, anxiously. "I'm afraid of being run over."

"If you are, you can sue 'em for damages," said Dick.

Finally Frank got safely over after several narrow escapes.

"Is it always so crowded?" he asked.

"A good deal worse sometimes," said Dick. "I knowed a young man once who waited six hours for a chance to cross, and at last got run over by an omnibus, leaving a widow and a large family of orphan children. His widow, a beautiful young woman, had to start a peanut and apple stand. There she is now."

"Where?"

Dick pointed to an apple stand close by. Behind it was a hideous old woman, of large proportions, wearing a huge bonnet.

Frank laughed.

"If that is the case," he said, "I think I will support her business."

"Leave it to me," said Dick, winking.

He advanced gravely to the apple stand, and said, "Old lady, have you paid your taxes?"

The astonished woman opened her eyes.

"I'm a gov'ment officer," said Dick, "sent by the mayor to collect your taxes. I'll take it in apples if you please. That big red one will about pay what you're owin' to the gov'ment."

"I don't know nothing about no taxes," said the old woman, in bewilderment.

"Then," said Dick, "I'll let you off this time. Give us two of your best apples, and my friend here, the President of the Common Council, will pay you."

Frank, smiling, paid three cents apiece for the apples, and they sauntered on.

Chatham Street, where they wished to go, was on the East side, so the two boys crossed the park. This park was about ten acres in size. Besides trees and grass, it contained several important public buildings. Dick pointed out City Hall, the Hall of Records, and the Rotunda.

"That's where the mayor's office is," said Dick. "Him and me are very good friends. I once blacked his boots by partic'lar appointment. That's the way I pay my city taxes."

CHAPTER 5

Chatham Street and Broadway

They were soon on Chatham Street, walking between rows of ready-made clothing shops. Many of the stores had half their merchandise displayed on the sidewalk. The owners stood at the doors of their shops, urging any passerby who even glanced at the goods to enter.

"Walk in, young gentlemen," said a stout man, at the entrance of one shop.

"No, I thank you," replied Dick, "as the fly said to the spider."

"We're selling off at less than cost."

"Of course you be. That's where you makes your money," said Dick.

The Chatham Street trader looked after Dick as if he didn't quite understand him. But Dick, without waiting for a reply, passed on with his companion.

"Clothes seem to be pretty cheap here," said Frank, noting the low prices on the signs.

"Yes, but Baxter Street is the cheapest place."

"Is it?"

"Yes. Johnny Nolan got a whole outfit there last week, for a dollar—coat, cap, vest, pants, and shoes."

"I will know where to come for clothes next time," said Frank, laughing. "I had no idea the city was so much cheaper than the country. I suppose the Baxter Street tailors are fashionable?"

"In course they are. Me and his honor, the mayor, always go there for clothes. When the mayor gets a new suit, I always have one made just like it," Dick said with a grin.

A little farther on a man was standing out on the sidewalk, distributing small printed handbills. Frank took one and read it:

"GRAND CLOSING-OUT SALE!—A variety of Beautiful and Costly Articles for Sale, at a Dollar apiece. Walk in, Gentlemen!"

"Whereabouts is this sale?" asked Frank.

"In here, young gentlemen," said a black-whiskered man, who appeared suddenly. "Walk in."

"Shall we go in, Dick?"

"It's a swindlin' shop," said Dick, in a low voice. "I've been there. That man's a regular cheat."

"Step in and see the articles," said the man, persuasively. "You needn't buy, you know."

"Are all the articles worth more'n a dollar?" asked Dick.

"Yes," said the other, "and some worth a great deal more."

"Such as what?"

"Well, there's a silver pitcher worth twenty dollars."

"And you sell it for a dollar. That's very kind of you," said Dick, innocently.

"Walk in, and you'll understand it."

"No, I guess not," said Dick. "My servants is so dishonest that I wouldn't like to trust 'em with a silver pitcher. Come along, Frank."

"How does he manage, Dick?" asked Frank, as they went on.

"All his articles are numbered, and he makes you pay a dollar, and then shakes some dice, and whatever the figgers come to, is the number of the article you draw. Most of 'em ain't worth ten cents."

They came to the hat store and Dick and Frank went in. For seventy-five cents, which Frank insisted on paying, Dick got a new cap. He did not think his old cap was worth keeping, so he dropped it onto a pile of trash outside the shop and walked on. When he looked back, he saw it picked up by a brother bootblack who appeared to feel it was better than his own.

They retraced their steps and went up Chambers Street to Broadway. At the corner of Broadway and Chambers Street was a large white marble building.

"What building is that?" Frank asked.

"That belongs to my friend A. T. Stewart," said Dick. "It's the biggest store on Broadway. If I ever retire from bootblackin', and go into business, I may buy him out, or build another store that'll take the shine off this one."

"That would be a very agreeable employment," said Frank, laughing.

The boys crossed to the west side of Broadway and walked slowly up the street. To Frank it was very interesting. Used to the quiet of the country, he was fascinated by the crowds of people on the sidewalks and the great variety of vehicles constantly passing in the street. The well-stocked shop windows particularly interested him.

"I don't see how so many shopkeepers can find people enough to buy all these things," he said. "We have only two stores in our village, and Broadway seems to be full of them."

"Yes," said Dick; "and it's pretty much the same on the avenues, 'specially the Third, Sixth, and Eighth Avenues. The Bowery, too, is a great place for shoppin'. There everybody sells cheaper'n anybody else, and nobody pretends to make no profit on their goods."

"Where's Barnum's Museum?" asked Frank.

"Oh, that's down nearly opposite the Astor House," said Dick. "Didn't you see a great building with lots of flags?"

"Yes."

"Well, that's Barnum's. They've got lions and bears and the World's Strongest Man and all kinds of interestin' things. It's a tip-top place. Haven't you ever been there?"

"No. I'll go if I get time," said Frank. "There is a boy at home who came to New York a month ago, and went to Barnum's and has been talking about it ever since, so I guess it must be worth seeing."

"You really ought to see it when you have time," Dick said.

"What building is that?" asked Frank, pointing to a structure set several yards back from the street.

"That is the New York Hospital," said Dick. "They're a rich institution, and take care of sick people on very reasonable terms."

"Did you ever go in there?"

"Yes," said Dick; "there was a friend of mine, Johnny Mullen, he was a newsboy, got run over by a omnibus as he was crossin' Broadway down near Park Place. He was carried to the Hospital, and me and some of his friends paid his board while he was there. It was only three dollars a week, which was very cheap, considerin' all the care they took of him. I come to see him while he was here. Everything looked so nice and comfortable that I thought about of coaxin' a omnibus driver to run over me so I might go there too."

"Did your friend have to have his leg cut off?"

asked Frank, interested.

"No," said Dick. "Johnny is around the streets as well as ever."

While this conversation was going on they reached No. 365, at the corner of Franklin Street.

"That's Taylor's Saloon," said Dick. "When I come into a fortune I will eat my meals there reg'lar."

"I have heard of it," said Frank. "They say it's very elegant. Suppose we go in and take an ice cream. It will give us a chance to see it better."

"Thank you," said Dick; "I think that's the most agreeable way of seein' the place myself."

The boys entered, and found themselves in a spacious and elegant room. The woodwork was painted gold and there were costly mirrors on all sides. They sat down to a small table with a marble top, and Frank gave the order.

"It reminds me of Aladdin's palace," said Frank, looking about him.

"Does it?" said Dick; "he must have had plenty of money."

"He had an old lamp, which he had only to rub, when the Genie would appear, and do whatever he wanted."

"That must have been a valuable lamp. I'd be willin' to give all my Erie Railroad shares for it."

The tall, thin man at the next table apparently heard this last remark of Dick's. Turning towards Dick, he said, "May I ask, young man, whether you are largely interested in this Erie Railroad?"

"I haven't got no property except what's invested in Erie," said Dick, with a comical side-glance at Frank.

"Indeed! I suppose the investment was made by your guardian."

"No," said Dick; "I manage my property myself."

"And I presume your dividends have not been large?"

"Why, no," said Dick; "you're about right there. They haven't."

"As I supposed. It's poor stock. Now, my young friend, I can recommend a much better investment, which will yield you a large annual income. I am agent of the Excelsior Copper Mining Company. It is one of the most productive mines in the world. It's sure to double whatever money you invest. All you have to do is to sell out your Erie shares, and invest in our stock, and I'll guarantee you a fortune in three years. How many shares did you say you had?"

"I didn't say, that I remember," said Dick. "Your offer is very kind. As soon as I get time I'll see about it."

"I hope you will," said the stranger. "Permit me to give you my card. I will be most happy to receive you at my office, where I can show you the maps of our mine."

"Very good," said Dick.

The stranger left the table and walked up to the desk to settle his bill.

"You see what it is to be a man of fortune, Frank," said Dick, "and wear good clothes. I wonder what that chap'll say when he sees me blackin' boots tomorrow in the street?"

"Perhaps you earn your money more honorably than he does, after all," said Frank. "Some of these mining companies are nothing but swindles, got up to cheat people out of their money."

"He's welcome to all he gets out of me," said Dick.

CHAPTER 6

Up Broadway to Madison Square

As the boys pursued their way up Broadway, Dick pointed out the elegant hotels and interesting buildings. At Eighth Street, Dick turned to the right and pointed out the Mercantile Library.

"My uncle told me about that. He said they have over fifty thousand books," Frank said. "Have you ever read any books?"

"No," said Dick; "I ain't much on readin'. It makes my head ache."

"I suppose you can't read very fast."

"I can read the little words pretty well, but the big ones is what stick me."

"If I lived in the city, I could teach you how to read better."

"Would you take so much trouble about me?" asked Dick, earnestly.

"Certainly. I'd like to see you getting on. There isn't much chance of that if you don't know how to read and write."

"You're very kind," said Dick, gratefully. "I wish you did live in New York. Whereabouts do you live?"

"About fifty miles off, in a town on the Hudson River. I wish you'd come up and see me sometime. I would like to have you come visit."

"Do you mean it?" asked Dick.

"Of course I do. Why shouldn't I?"

"What would your folks say if they knowed you asked a bootblack to visit you?"

"You are none the worse for being a boot-black, Dick."

"I ain't used to genteel society," said Dick. "I wouldn't know how to behave."

"Then I could show you. You won't be a bootblack all your life, you know."

"No," said Dick; "I'm goin' to knock off when I get to be ninety."

"Before that, I hope," said Frank, smiling.

"I really wish I could get somethin' else to do," said Dick, seriously. "I'd like to be a office boy, and learn business, and grow up 'spectable."

"Why don't you try, and see if you can get a place, Dick?"

"Who'd hire Ragged Dick?"

"But you ain't ragged now, Dick."

"No," said Dick; "I look a little better than I did in my Washington coat. But if I got a job in a office, they wouldn't give me more'n three dollars a week, and I couldn't live 'spectable on that."

"No, I suppose not," said Frank, thoughtfully.

"But you would get more at the end of the first year."

"Yes," said Dick; "but by that time I'd be nothin' but skin and bones."

Frank laughed. "Whereabouts are we now?" he asked, as they emerged from Fourth Avenue into Union Square.

"That is Union Park," said Dick. In front of them was a beautiful park with a pond in the center. There was also a large statue of a military figure on a horse.

"Is that the statue of General Washington?" asked Frank.

"Yes," said Dick. "He's growed some since he was President. If he'd been as tall as that when he fought in the Revolution, he'd have walloped the Britishers some, I reckon."

Looking up at the fourteen-foot statue, Frank asked, "How about the coat, Dick? Would it fit you?"

"Well, it might be rather loose," said Dick, "I ain't much more'n ten feet high with my boots off."

"No, I should think not," said Frank, smiling. "You're a funny boy, Dick."

"Well, I've been brought up funny. Some boys is born with a silver spoon in their mouth. The Queen of England's boys is born with a gold spoon, set with diamonds. But gold and silver was scarce when I was born, and mine was pewter."

"Perhaps the gold and silver will come in time, Dick. Did you ever hear of Dick Whittington?"

"Never did. Was he a Ragged Dick?"

"I shouldn't wonder if he was. At any rate he was very poor when he was a boy, but he didn't stay so. Before he died, he became Lord Mayor of London."

"Did he?" asked Dick, looking interested. "How did he do it?"

"Why, you see, a rich merchant took pity on him and gave him a home in his own house. Soon after, the merchant was going to send a ship to foreign lands. Dick was very clever. And he worked hard to earn and save money. With the help of the merchant, he prospered as he grew up. In time he became a very rich merchant himself, respected by all, and eventually he was elected Lord Mayor of London."

"That's a pretty good story," said Dick. "But I don't know any rich merchants to help me out."

"No, but you may rise in some other way. Many distinguished men were once poor boys. There's hope for you, Dick, if you'll try."

"Nobody ever talked to me like this before," said Dick. "They just called me Ragged Dick, and told me I'd grow up to be a loafer and come to the gallows."

"My telling you so won't make it turn out so, Dick. If you'll try to be somebody, and grow up into a respectable member of society, you will. You may not become rich—it isn't everybody that becomes rich, you know—but you can obtain a good position and be respected."

"I'll try," said Dick, earnestly. "I wouldn't have been Ragged Dick this long if I hadn't spent my money in goin' to the theater, and treatin' boys to oyster-stews, and bettin' money on cards, and such like."

"Have you lost money that way?"

"Lots of it. One time I saved up five dollars to buy me a new suit, when Limpy Jim wanted me to play a game with him."

"Limpy Jim?" said Frank.

"Yes, he's lame. That's what makes us call him Limpy Jim."

"I suppose you lost?"

"Yes, I lost every penny, and had to sleep out, 'cause I hadn't a cent to pay for lodgin'. 'Twas a awful cold night, and I got most froze."

"Wouldn't Jim let you have any of the money he had won to pay for a lodging?"

"No; I asked him for five cents, but he wouldn't let me have it."

"Can you get lodging for five cents?" asked Frank, in surprise.

"Yes," said Dick, "but not at the Fifth Avenue Hotel. That's it right over there."

CHAPTER 7

The Wallet

They had reached the intersection of Broadway and Fifth Avenue. Before them was a beautiful park of ten acres. On the left-hand side was a large marble building. This was the building at which Dick pointed.

"Is that the Fifth Avenue Hotel?" asked Frank. "I've heard about it. My Uncle William always stops there when he comes to New York."

"I once slept outside of it," said Dick. "They was very reasonable in their charges and told me I might come again."

"Perhaps sometime you'll be able to sleep inside," said Frank.

"I guess that'll be when Queen Victoria goes to the Five Points to live."

"It looks like a palace," said Frank. "The queen needn't be ashamed to live in a beautiful building like that."

At that moment a gentleman passed them on

the sidewalk. He looked back at Dick, as if his face seemed familiar.

"I know that man," said Dick, after he had passed. "He's one of my customers."

"What is his name?"

"I don't know."

"He looked back as if he thought he knew you."

"He would have knowed me at once if it hadn't been for my new clothes," said Dick. "I don't look much like Ragged Dick now."

"I suppose your face looked familiar."

"All but the dirt," said Dick, laughing. "I don't always have the chance of washing my face and hands in the Astor House."

"You told me," said Frank, "that there was a place where you could get a bed for five cents. Where's that?"

"It's the News-boys' Lodgin' House, on Fulton Street," said Dick, "up over the *Sun* newspaper office. It's a good place. I don't know what us boys would do without it. They give you supper for six cents, and a bed for five cents more."

"I suppose some boys don't even have the five cents to pay, do they?"

"They'll trust the boys," said Dick. "But I don't like to get trusted. I'd be ashamed to get trusted for five cents, or ten either. One night I was comin' down Chatham Street, with fifty cents in my pocket. I was goin' to get a good oyster-stew, and then go to the lodgin' house. But somehow it slipped through a hole in my pocket, and I hadn't a cent left. If it had been summer I wouldn't have cared, but it's rather tough stayin' out winter nights."

"What did you do?" Frank asked.

"I went to the *Times* office. I knowed one of the pressmen, and he let me set down in a corner, where I was warm, and I soon got fast asleep."

"Why don't you get a room somewhere and so always have a home to go to?"

"I dunno," said Dick. "I never thought of it. P'rhaps I may hire a furnished house on Madison Square."

While this conversation was going on, they had turned into Twenty-fifth Street. They had just reached Third Avenue when they noticed a man in front of them stop suddenly. He bent over and appeared to pick up something from the sidewalk. Then he looked around in rather a confused way.

"I know his game," whispered Dick. "Come on and you'll see what it is."

He hurried Frank forward until they overtook the man, who had come to a standstill.

"Have you found anything?" asked Dick.

"Yes," said the man, "I found this."

He held up a wallet which seemed stuffed with bills.

"Whew!" exclaimed Dick. "You're in luck."

"I suppose somebody lost it," said the man, "and will offer a large reward."

"Which you'll get."

"Unfortunately I must take the next train to Boston. I haven't time to hunt up the owner."

"Then I suppose you'll take the wallet with you," said Dick, innocently.

"I would like to leave it with some honest fellow who will return it to the owner," said the man, glancing at the boys.

"I'm honest," said Dick.

"I've no doubt of it," said the man. "Well, young man, I'll make you an offer. You take the wallet—"

"All right. Hand it over, then."

"Wait a minute. There must be a large sum inside. There might be a thousand dollars in it. The owner will probably give you a hundred dollars reward."

"Why don't you stay and get it?" asked Frank.

"I would, but my wife is sick, and I must get home to Boston as soon as possible. Just give me twenty dollars, and I'll hand you the wallet, and let you make whatever you can by returning it. Come, that's a good offer. What do you say?"

"Twenty dollars is a good deal of money," said Dick, appearing to hesitate.

"You'll get it back, and a good deal more," said the stranger.

"I don't know. What would you do, Frank?"

"Maybe you should do it," said Frank, "if you've got the money." He was surprised to think that Dick had so much on him.

"Maybe I will," said Dick, after some hesitation. "I guess I won't lose much."

"You can't lose anything," said the stranger briskly. "Only be quick, for I must be on my way to the train."

Dick pulled out a bill from his pocket and handed it to the stranger, receiving the wallet in return. At that moment a policeman turned the corner. The stranger thrust the bill into his pocket without looking at it and walked quickly away.

"What's in the wallet, Dick?" asked Frank. "I hope there's enough to repay the money you gave him."

Dick laughed and said, "I imagine there is."

"But you gave him twenty dollars. That's a good deal of money."

"If I had given him as much as that, I deserve to be cheated out of it."

"But you did—didn't you?"

"He thought so."

"What did you give him?"

"It was nothing but an ad for a store made up to imitate a bank-bill."

"You shouldn't to have cheated him, Dick," Frank said, seriously.

"Didn't he want to cheat me?"

"I don't know."

"What do you s'pose is in this wallet?" asked Dick, holding it up.

Frank looked at the stuffed wallet and answered, "Money, and a good deal of it."

"There ain't money enough in it to buy a oyster-stew," said Dick. "If you don't believe it, just look while I open it."

So saying he opened the wallet and showed Frank that it was stuffed with pieces of blank paper, carefully folded up in the shape of bills.

Frank, who had never heard of the "drop-game," looked amazed.

"I guess I got the best of him there," Dick said. "This wallet's worth somethin'. I'll use it to keep my certificates of Erie stock in, and all my other papers that ain't of no use to anybody but the owner."

"That's the kind of papers it's got in it now," said Frank, smiling.

"That's so!" said Dick.

"Well look at that!" he exclaimed suddenly. "If there ain't the old chap comin' back ag'in. He looks as if he'd heard bad news from his sick wife."

By this time the wallet dropper had come up to them. He said to Dick in an undertone, "Give me back that wallet, you young rascal!"

"Beg your pardon, mister," said Dick, "but was you addressin' me?"

"Yes, I was."

"'You called me by the wrong name. I've knowed some rascals, but I ain't got the honor to belong to the family."

He looked innocently at the other as he spoke, which didn't improve the man's temper. Being used to swindling others, the man did not like having someone swindle him.

"Give me back that wallet," he repeated in a threatening voice.

"Couldn't do it," said Dick, coolly. "I'm go'n' to restore it to the owner. The contents is so valuable that I'm certain I'll get a reward."

"You gave me a fake bill," said the man. "You've swindled me."

"I thought it was the other way."

"None of your nonsense," said the man angrily. "If you don't give up that wallet, I'll call a policeman."

"I wish you would," said Dick. "They might know whose wallet it is and can return it."

The "dropper" was irritated by Dick's refusal and by casual manner. "Do you want to spend the night in the Tombs jail?" he asked.

"Thank you for your very kind proposal," said

Dick; "but it ain't convenient to-day. Any other time, when you'd like to have me come and visit you, I'd be happy to. But my two youngest children is down with the measles, and I expect I'll have to set up all night to take care of 'em. Is the Tombs, in general, a pleasant place of residence?"

Dick asked this question with such earnestness that Frank could scarcely keep from laughing. The dropper, however, did not find it so amusing.

"You'll know sometime," he said, scowling.

"I'll make you a fair offer," said Dick. "If I get more'n fifty dollars as a reward for my honesty, I'll divide it with you. But I say, ain't it time to go back to your sick family in Boston?"

Deciding he would get nowhere with Dick, the man strode away muttering curses.

"You were too smart for him, Dick," said Frank.

"Yes," said Dick, "I ain't knocked round the city streets all my life for nothin'."

CHAPTER 8

Dick's Early History

Have you always lived in New York, Dick?" asked Frank, after a pause.

"Ever since I can remember."

"Have you got any father or mother?"

"I ain't got no mother. She died when I was three years old. My father went to sea; but he went off before mother died, and nothin' was ever heard of him. I expect he got wrecked, or died at sea."

"And what happened to you when your mother died?"

"The folks she boarded with took care of me, but they was poor, and they couldn't do much. When I was seven the woman died, and her husband went out West, and then I had to scratch for myself."

"At seven years old!" exclaimed Frank, in amazement.

"Yes," said Dick, "I was a little feller to take care of myself."

"What did you do?"

"Sometimes one thing, and sometimes another," said Dick. "I changed my business accordin' as I had to. Sometimes I was a newsboy, but I give it up after a while."

"What for?"

"Well, they didn't always put news enough in their papers, and people wouldn't buy 'em as fast as I wanted 'em to. So one mornin' I was stuck on a lot of *Herald Tribunes*, and I thought I'd make a sensation. So I called out 'GREAT NEWS! QUEEN OF ENGLAND ASSASSINATED!' All my *Heralds* went off like hot cakes, and I went off, too. But one of the gentlemen what got sold remembered me, and said he'd have me arrested. That's what made me change my business."

"That wasn't right, Dick," said Frank.

"I know it," said Dick; "but lots of boys does it."

"That don't make it any better."

"No," said Dick, "I was sort of ashamed at the time, 'specially about one poor old gentleman—a Englishman he was. He couldn't help cryin' to think the queen was dead. His hands shook when he handed me the money for the paper."

"What did you do next?"

"I went into the match business," said Dick. "But it was small sales and small profits. Most of the people I called on had just laid in a stock, and didn't want to buy. So one cold night, when I hadn't money enough to pay for a lodgin', I burned the last of my matches to keep me from freezin'. But it cost too much to get warm that way, and I couldn't keep it up."

"You've seen hard times, Dick," said Frank.

"Yes," said Dick, "I've knowed what it was to be hungry and cold, with nothin' to eat or to warm me; but there's one thing I never could do."

"What's that?"

"I never stole," said Dick. "It's mean and I wouldn't do it."

"Were you ever tempted to?"

"Lots of times. Once I had been goin' round all day, and hadn't sold any matches, except three cents' worth early in the mornin'. With that I bought an apple, thinkin' I should get some more soon. When evenin' come I was awful hungry. I went into a baker's just to look at the bread. It made me feel kind o' good just to look at the bread and cakes, and I thought maybe they would give me some. I asked 'em wouldn't they give me a loaf, and take their pay in matches. But they said they'd got enough matches to last three months; so there wasn't any chance for a trade. While I was standin' at the stove warmin' me, the baker went into a back room, and I felt so hungry I thought I would take just one loaf, and go off with it. There was such a big pile I don't think he'd have known it."

"But you didn't do it?"

"No, I didn't and I was glad of it. When the man came in ag'in, he said he wanted some one to carry some cake to a lady in St. Mark's Place. His boy was sick, and he hadn't no one to send. So he told me he'd give me ten cents if I would go. I went, and when I come back, I took my pay in bread and cakes. Didn't they taste good, though?"

"So you didn't stay long in the match business, Dick?"

"No, I couldn't sell enough to make it pay. Then there was some folks that wanted me to sell cheaper to them; so I couldn't make any profit. There was one old lady—she was rich, too, for she lived in a big brick house—beat me down so, that I didn't make no profit at all. But she would only buy at her price, and I hadn't sold none that day; so I let her have them. I don't see why rich folks should be so hard upon a poor boy that wants to make a livin'."

"There's a good deal of meanness in the world, I'm afraid, Dick."

"If everybody was like you and your uncle," said Dick, "there would be some chance for poor people. If I was rich I'd try to help 'em along."

"Maybe you will be rich sometime, Dick."

Dick shook his head. "I'm afraid all my wallets will be like this," said Dick, holding up the one he had gotten from the dropper.

"That depends very much on yourself, Dick," said Frank. "The man who owns Stewart's Department Store wasn't always rich, you know."

"Wasn't he?"

"When he first came to New York as a young man he was a teacher, and teachers are not gener-

ally very rich. At last he went into business, starting in a small way, and worked his way up by
degrees. But there was one thing he determined in
the beginning: that he would be honorable in all
his dealings, and never overreach any one for the
sake of making money. If there was a chance for
him, Dick, there is a chance for you."

"He knowedF enough to be a teacher. I'm
awful ignorant," said Dick.

"But you don't have to stay ignorant."

"How can I help it?"

"Can't you learn at school?"

"I can't go to school 'cause I've got my livin'
to earn. It wouldn't do me much good if I learned
to read and write and just as I'd got learned I
starved to death."

"But aren't there night schools?"

"Yes."

"Why don't you go? I suppose you don't work
in the evenings."

"I never cared much about it," said Dick, "and
that's the truth. But since I've got to talkin' with
you, I'll think more about it. I guess I'll begin to
go."

"I wish you would, Dick. You'll make a smart
man if you only get a little education."

"Do you think so?" asked Dick.

"I know so. A boy who has earned his own living since he was seven years old must have something in him. You've had a hard time of it so far in
life, but I think better times are in store. I feel sure

you can do well if you only try."

"You're a good fellow," said Dick. "I'm afraid I'm a pretty rough customer, but I ain't as bad as some. I mean to turn over a new leaf and try to grow up 'spectable. I'm willin' to work hard."

"And you must not only work hard, but also work in the right way."

"What's the right way?"

"You began in the right way when you decided never to steal, or do anything mean or dishonorable. That will make people have confidence in you when they come to know you. But, in order to succeed well, you must manage to get as good an education as you can. Until you do, you cannot get a position in an office, even to run errands."

"That's so," said Dick. "I never thought how awful ignorant I was till now."

"That can be fixed with hard work," said Frank. "A year will do a great deal for you.'"

"I'll see what I can do," said Dick, energetically.

CHAPTER 9

A Scene in a Horse-car

The boys had turned onto Third Avenue.

"Now," said Dick, "where shall we go?"

"I would like to see Central Park," said Frank. "Is it far off?"

"It is about a mile and a half from here," said Dick. "This is Twenty-ninth Street, and the Park begins at Fifty-ninth Street."

Dick went on to explain that a ways north of City Hall the cross-streets begin to be numbered in regular order. "Central Park," he said, "runs between Fifty-ninth Street and One Hundred and Tenth Street. It'll only cost us six cents to ride there in the horse-cars."

"All right then," Frank said. "We'll jump aboard the next car."

A car was approaching, but it seemed pretty crowded.

"Shall we take that, or wait for another?" asked Frank.

"The next'll most likely be as bad," said Dick. The boys signalled to the conductor to stop and got on the front platform. They had to stand up till the car reached Fortieth Street, when several passengers got off.

A middle-aged woman with an unpleasant expression on her face was seated near where they were standing. When the two gentlemen who sat beside her got up, she spread her skirts to fill two seats. Disregarding this, the boys sat down.

"There ain't room for two," she said, looking sourly at Frank.

"There were two here before."

"Well, there ought not to have been. Some people like to crowd in where they're not wanted."

"And some like to take up a double allowance of room," thought Frank. But he did not say so. He saw that the woman had a bad temper and thought it wisest to say nothing.

Frank began looking out the car windows with great interest. He supposed he would have nothing further to do with the woman beside him. But he was mistaken.

While he was busy looking out of the car window, she plunged her hand into her pocket in search of her purse, but she was unable to find it. Instantly she jumped to the conclusion that it had been stolen, and her suspicions fastened on Frank.

"Conductor!" she exclaimed in a sharp voice.

"What is it, ma'am?" asked the conductor.

"My purse has been stolen. There was four dollars and eighty cents in it. I know, because I counted it when I paid my fare."

"Who stole it?"

"That boy," she said pointing to Frank. "He crowded in here on purpose to rob me, and I want you to search him right off."

"That's a lie!" exclaimed Dick, indignantly. Frank was too astonished to say anything at first.

"Oh, you're in league with him, I dare say," said the woman spitefully. "You're as bad as he is, I'll be bound."

"You're a nice female, you be!" said Dick, ironically.

"Don't you dare to call me a female, sir," said the lady, furiously.

"Why, you ain't a man in disguise, are you?" said Dick.

By this time, Frank had recovered himself. "You are very much mistaken, madam," he said quietly. "The conductor may search me, if you wish."

A charge of theft, made in a crowded car, of course made quite a sensation. Cautious passengers instinctively put their hands on their pockets, to make sure that they, too, had not been robbed. As for Frank, his face flushed, and he felt indignant that he should even be suspected of such a crime.

Dick, on the contrary, thought it a great joke that such a charge should have been made against his companion.

Meanwhile the passengers sided with the boys. Appearances go a great ways, and Frank did not look like a thief.

"I think you must be mistaken, madam," said a gentleman sitting opposite. "The lad does not look as if he would steal."

"You can't tell by looks," said the lady, sourly. "They're deceitful; thieves are generally well dressed."

"Be they?" said Dick. "You ought to see me with my Washington coat on. You'd think I was the biggest thief ever you saw."

"I've no doubt you are," said the lady, scowling at him.

"Thank you, ma'am," said Dick. "'Tisn't often I get such fine compliments."

"None of your impudence," said the lady, angrily.

Meanwhile the car had stopped.

"How long are we going to stop here?" demanded a passenger, impatiently. "I'm in a hurry, if none of the rest of you are."

"I want my purse," said the lady, defiantly.

"Well, ma'am, I haven't got it, and I don't see as it's doing you any good keeping us all here."

"Conductor, will you call a policeman to search that young scamp?" continued the lady. "You don't expect I'm going to lose my money and do nothing about it."

"I'll turn my pockets inside out if you want me to," said Frank, proudly. "There's no need of a policeman. The conductor, or any one else, may search me."

"Well, youngster," said the conductor, "if the lady agrees, I'll search you."

The lady nodded in agreement.

Frank turned his pockets inside out, but they contained nothing was but his own wallet and a penknife.

"Well, ma'am, are you satisfied?" asked the conductor.

"No, I ain't," said she, decidedly.

"You don't think he's got it still?"

"No, but he's passed it over to the other one, that boy there that's so full of impudence."

"That's me," said Dick, comically.

"He confesses it," said the lady; "I want him searched."

"All right," said Dick, "I'm ready for the operation, only, I've got valuable property on me. Be careful not to drop any of my Erie Bonds."

Dick emptied his pockets. They contained a rusty jack-knife, about fifty cents in change, and the bulging walled he had gotten from the swindler.

The conductor held up the wallet. It's size caused amazement among the other passengers.

"It seems to me you carry a large wallet for a young man of your age," said the conductor.

"That's what I carry my cash and valuable papers in," said Dick.

"I suppose that isn't yours, ma'am," said the conductor, turning to the lady.

"No," said she, scornfully. "I wouldn't carry round such a wallet as that. Most likely he's stolen it from somebody else."

"What a prime detective you'd be!" said Dick. "P'rhaps you know who I took it from."

"Maybe my money's in it," said the lady, sharply. "Conductor, will you open that wallet, and see what there is in it?"

"Don't disturb the valuable papers," said Dick, in a tone of pretended anxiety.

The contents of the wallet excited some amusement among the passengers.

"There don't seem to be much money here," said the conductor, taking out a roll of tissue paper cut out in the shape of bills, and rolled up.

"No," said Dick. "Didn't I tell you them were papers of no value to anybody but the owner? If the lady'd like to borrow, I won't charge no interest."

"Where is my money, then?" said the lady, uneasily. "I wouldn't be surprised if one of the young scamps had thrown it out of the window."

"You'd better search your pocket once more," said the gentleman opposite. "I don't believe either of the boys is in fault. They don't look to me as if they would steal."

"Thank you, sir" said Frank.

The lady followed out the suggestion, and, plunging her hand once more into her pocket, drew out a small purse. She hardly knew whether to be glad or sorry at this discovery. It placed her in rather an awkward position after the fuss she had made for nothing.

"Is that the purse you thought stolen?" asked the conductor.

"Yes," said she, rather confusedly.

"Then you've been keeping me waiting all this time for nothing," he said, sharply. "I wish you'd take care to be sure next time before you make such a disturbance for nothing. I've lost five minutes and am now running late."

"I can't help it," was the cross reply; "I didn't know it was in my pocket."

"It seems to me you owe an apology to the boys you accused of a theft which they have not committed," said the gentleman opposite.

"I won't apologize to anybody," said the lady. "Least of all to such whipper-snappers as they are."

"Thank you, ma'am," said Dick, comically; "your handsome apology is accepted."

"You're a character," said the gentleman, with a smile.

"A bad character!" muttered the lady.

The car had now reached Fifty-ninth Street, the southern boundary of Central Park.

"You'd better look out for pickpockets, my lad," said the conductor, pleasantly as they were getting off. "That big wallet of yours might prove a great temptation."

"That's so," said Dick. "That's the misfortin' of being rich. Astor and me don't sleep much for fear of burglars breakin' in and robbin' us of our valuable treasures. Sometimes I think I'll give all my money to an orphanage."

The car rolled away, and the boys turned up Fifty-ninth Street, for two long blocks still separated them from the Park.

CHAPTER 10

A Victim of Misplaced Confidence

"**W**hat a character you are, Dick!" said Frank, laughing. "You always seem to be in good spirits."

"No, I ain't always. Sometimes I have the blues."

"When?"

"Well, once last winter it was awful cold, and there was big holes in my shoes, and my gloves and all my warm clothes was at the tailor's. I felt as if life was sort of tough, and I'd like it if some rich man would adopt me, and give me plenty to eat and drink and wear. Sometimes it's discouragin' to think nobody cares about you."

"Don't say that, Dick," Frank said. "I care about you."

"You do?"

"Yes."

"That's good to know," said Dick, earnestly. "It's good to know that I have one friend who cares about me."

By now they had arrived at Central Park.

Frank looked at piles of dirt and rocks. Workmen drove wagons along muddy cart tracks. The only buildings along the edge of the park were some temporary huts used by the workers.

"If this is Central Park," said Frank, "I don't think much of it. My father's got a large pasture that is much nicer."

"It'll look better some time," said Dick. "There ain't much to see now but rocks. They've only just started work on it. We will take a walk over it if you want to."

"No," said Frank, "I've seen as much of it as I want to."

"Then we'll go back. We can take the Sixth Avenue horse-car. That will bring us out at Vesey Street just beside the Astor House."

In about three-quarters of an hour the boys got out of the horse-car beside the Astor House.

"Are you goin' in now, Frank?" asked Dick.

"That depends upon whether you have anything else to show me."

"Wouldn't you like to go to Wall Street?"

"Isn't that the street where there are so many bankers and stock brokers?"

"Yes, I s'pose you ain't afraid of bulls and bears, are you?"

"Bulls and bears?" said Frank, puzzled. "What do you mean?"

"When the stocks go up, they say it's a bull market. And when they go down, it's a the bear market."

"Oh, I see. Yes, I'd like to go."

They walked down Broadway as far as Trinity Church and then entered a narrow street.

"This is Wall Street," said Dick.

"This little street is where all those vast amounts of money get passed around?" asked Frank. Then, pointing to a large marble building with columns, he said, "This looks like pictures I've seen of Greek temples from two thousand years ago. What's this building?"

"That's the Custom House," said Dick.

"I've heard of that. That's where they collect the taxes for all the things brought in on ships."

As they stood at the foot of the granite steps looking up at the entrance, a tall young man came up to them. It was evident from his clothing that he was not from the city. He was holding a piece of paper and he looked confused and anxious.

"Be they a-payin' out money inside there?" he asked, gesturing toward the Custom House.

"I guess so," said Dick. "Are you a-goin' in for some?"

"Wal, yes. I've got an order here for sixty dollars. I made a kind of speculation this morning."

"What do you mean?" asked Frank.

"Wal, you see I brought down some money to put in the bank. Fifty dollars it was. I hadn't justly made up my mind what bank to put it into, when a man came up in a terrible hurry. He said it was very unfortunate, but the bank wasn't open, and he must have some money right off. He had to go out of the city by the next train. I asked him how much he wanted. He said fifty dollars. I told him I'd got that, and he offered me a check on the bank for sixty, and I let him have it. I thought that was a pretty easy way to earn ten dollars, so I counted out the money and he went off. He told me I'd hear a bell ring when they began to pay out money. But I've waited most two hours, and I ain't heard it yet. I'd ought to be goin', for I told dad I'd be home tonight. Do you think I can get the money now?"

"Will you show me the check?" asked Frank, suspecting the young man had been swindled.

The check was written on the "Washington Bank," in the sum of sixty dollars, and was signed "Ephraim Smith."

"Washington Bank!" repeated Frank. "Dick, is there such a bank in the city?"

"Not as I knows on," said Dick.

"Ain't this the Washington Bank?" asked the young man.

"No, it's the Custom House."

"And won't they give me any money for this?" asked the young man, the perspiration standing on his brow.

"I am afraid the man who gave it to you was a swindler," said Frank, gently.

"And won't I ever see my fifty dollars again?" asked the youth in agony.

"I am afraid not."

"What'll dad say?" cried the miserable youth.

"It makes me feel sick to think of it. I wish I had the feller here. I'd shake him out of his boots."

"What did he look like? I'll call a policeman and you can describe him. Perhaps in that way you can get track of your money."

Dick called a policeman, who listened to the description and recognized the operator as an experienced swindler. He assured the young man that there was very little chance of his ever seeing his money again. The boys left the miserable youth loudly bewailing his bad luck and continued on their way down the street.

"He's a baby," said Dick, contemptuously. "He'd ought to know how to take care of himself and his money. A feller has to look sharp in this city, or he'll lose his eye-teeth before he knows it."

"I suppose you never got swindled out of fifty dollars, Dick?"

"No, I don't carry no such small bills," he replied.

"You're a character, Dick. What's that building there at the end of the street?"

"That's the Wall-Street Ferry to Brooklyn."

"How long does it take to go across?"

"Not more'n five minutes."

"Suppose we just ride over and back."

"All right!" said Dick. "It's rather expensive; but if you don't mind, I don't."

"Why, how much does it cost?"

"Two cents apiece."

"I guess I can stand that. Let us go."

They paid the fare and were soon on the ferry-boat, bound for Brooklyn.

They had scarcely entered the boat, when Dick, pointed to a man just outside of the main cabin.

"Do you see that man, Frank?" he asked.

"Yes, what of him?"

"He's the man that cheated the country chap out of his fifty dollars."

CHAPTER 11

Dick as a Detective

"**W**hat makes you think that's the man who swindled the boy?" Frank asked.

"Because I've seen him before, and I know he's up to them kind of tricks. When I heard how he looked, I was sure I knowed him."

"Our recognizing him won't be of much use," said Frank. "It won't get back the money."

"I don't know," said Dick, thoughtfully. "May be I can get it."

"How?" asked Frank, incredulously.

"Wait a minute, and you'll see."

Dick left his companion and went up to the man.

"Ephraim Smith," said Dick in a low voice.

The man turned suddenly and looked at Dick uneasily.

"What did you say?" he asked.

"I believe your name is Ephraim Smith," continued Dick.

"You're mistaken," said the man, about to

move off.

"Stop a minute," said Dick. "Don't you keep your money in the Washington Bank?"

"I don't know any such bank. I'm in a hurry, young man, and I can't stop to answer any foolish questions."

The boat had by this time reached the Brooklyn pier, and Mr. Ephraim Smith seemed in a hurry to land.

"Look here," said Dick; "you'd better not go on shore unless you want to jump into the arms of a policeman."

"What do you mean?" asked the man, startled.

"That little affair of yours is known to the police," said Dick; "about how you got fifty dollars out of a greenhorn on a false check. It may not be safe for you to go ashore."

"I don't know what you're talking about," said the swindler.

"Yes, you do," said Dick. "There isn't but one thing to do. Just give me back that money, and I'll see that you're not touched. If you don't, I'll give you up to the first policeman we meet."

Dick looked so determined and spoke so confidently that the other, overcome by his fears, no longer hesitated, but passed a roll of bills to Dick and hastily left the boat.

All this Frank witnessed with amazement.

"How did you do it?" he asked eagerly .

Dick explained what had happened and then said, "Now we'll go back and carry the money."

"Suppose we don't find the young man?"

"Then the p'lice will take care of it."

They remained on board the boat and in five minutes were again in New York. Going up Wall Street, they met the young man not far from the Custom House. His face showed how upset he was.

"Hello!" said Dick. "Have you found your money?"

"No," gasped the young man. "I won't ever see it again. The mean skunk's cheated me out of it. It took me most six months to save it up. I was workin' for Deacon Pinkham in our place. Oh, I wish I'd never come to New York! The deacon, he told me he'd keep it for me; but I wanted to put it in the bank, and now it's all gone!"

The miserable youth was on the verge of tears.

"I say," said Dick, "take a look at what I've got here."

When the youth saw his lost treasure he was overjoyed. He seized Dick's hand and shook it with so much energy that Dick began to feel alarmed for its safety.

"'It 'pears to me you take my arm for a pump-handle," said he. "Couldn't you show your gratitude some other way? It's just possible I may want to use my arm ag'in some time."

The young man looked embarrassed and let go of Dick's hand. "I can't thank you enough," he said.

"All right," said Dick. "You just hang onto that money. Don't go takin' no more checks for it!"

"You bet I won't," said the youth.

Frank and Dick walked back up Wall Street toward Broadway, the youth calling out his thanks after them.

"I think I ought to go back to the Astor House. My uncle has probably returned by now."

"All right," said Dick.

The two boys walked up to Broadway, just where the tall steeple of Trinity faces the street of bankers and brokers, and walked leisurely to the hotel. When they arrived at the Astor House, Dick said, "Goodbye, Frank."

"Not yet," said Frank; "I want you to come in with me."

Dick followed him up the steps. Frank went to the reading room, where he found his uncle reading a copy of *The Evening Post*.

"Well, boys," he said, looking up, "have you had a pleasant day?"

"Yes, sir," said Frank. "Dick's a terrific guide."

"So this is Dick," said Mr. Whitney, looking at him with a smile. "Upon my word, I would hardly have known him. I must congratulate him on his improved appearance."

"Frank's been very kind to me," said Dick.

"I believe he is a good boy," said Mr. Whitney. "I hope, Dick, you will prosper in the world. With hard work and a bit of luck, a man can advance in life. I haven't risen very high myself, but I have met with moderate success in life. But there was a time when I was as poor as you."

"Were you, sir?" asked Dick, eagerly.

"Yes, my boy, there were times I had to go without my dinner because I didn't have enough money to pay for it."

"How did you move up in the world?" asked Dick, anxiously.

"I started in a printing-office as an apprentice and worked for some years. Then my eyes gave out and I had to give that up. Not knowing what else to do, I went into the country and worked on a farm. After a while I was lucky enough to invent a machine, which has brought me in a great deal of money. But there was one thing I got while I was in the printing-office which I value more than money."

"What was that, sir?"

"A taste for reading and study. During my spare hours I improved myself by study. It was one of my books that first put me on the track of the invention. So you see, my lad, that my studious habits paid me in money, as well as in another way."

"I'm awful ignorant," said Dick.

"But you are young, and, I judge, a smart boy. If you try to learn, you can, and if you ever expect to do anything in the world, you must know something of books."

"I will," said Dick. "I ain't always goin' to black boots for a livin'."

"All labor is respectable, my lad, and you have no cause to be ashamed of any honest business. But when you can get something to do that promises better future, I advise you to take hold of it. Till then earn your living in the way you are used to, avoid extravagance, and save up a little money if you can."

"Thank you for your advice," said Dick. "There ain't many that takes an interest in Ragged Dick."

"So that's your name," said Mr. Whitney. "If I judge you rightly, it won't be long before you change it. Save your money, my lad, buy books, and determine to be somebody, and you may yet fill an honorable position."

"I'll try," said Dick. "Good-night, sir."

"Wait a minute, Dick," said Frank. "Your blacking-box and old clothes are upstairs. You may want them."

"In course," said Dick. "I couldn't get along without my best clothes and the tools of my trade."

"Go along with Frank and get your things," said Mr. Whitney. "But I want to see you, Dick, before you go."

"Yes, sir," said Dick.

"Where are you going to sleep tonight, Dick?" asked Frank, as they went upstairs together.

"P'rhaps at the Fifth Avenue Hotel—on the outside," said Dick.

"Haven't you any place to sleep, then?"

"There's always the box I slept in last night."

"Don't you earn enough to pay for a room, Dick?"

"Yes," said Dick. "Only I spend my money

foolish, goin' to the Old Bowery and sometimes gamblin' in Baxter Street."

"You won't gamble any more, —will you, Dick?" said Frank.

"No, I won't," said Dick.

"You'll promise?"

"Yes, and I'll keep it. You're a good feller. I wish you was goin' to be in New York."

"I am going to a boarding-school in Connecticut. The name of the town is Barnton. Will you write to me, Dick?"

"My writing would look like hens' tracks," said Dick.

"Never mind. I want you to write. When you write you can tell me where to write you, and I'll send you a letter."

"I wish you would," said Dick.

After they had collected Dick's clothes and box, they went back to the reading room.

"Uncle, Dick's ready to go," said Frank.

"Goodbye, my lad," said Mr. Whitney. "I hope to hear good accounts of you sometime. Don't forget what I have told you. Remember that your future position depends mainly upon yourself, and that it will be high or low as you choose to make it."

Mr. Whitney then held out a five-dollar bill. Dick shrunk back.

"I don't like to take it," he said. "I haven't earned it."

"Perhaps not," said Mr. Whitney; "but I give

it to you because I remember my own friendless youth. I hope it may be useful to you. Sometime when you are a prosperous man, you can repay it by helping to some poor boy who is struggling upward as you are now."

"I will, sir," said Dick.

He no longer refused the money, but took it gratefully. Then, saying goodbye to Frank and his uncle, he went out into the street. A feeling of loneliness came over him as he left Frank. He had developed a strong feeling of friendship in the few hours he had known him.

CHAPTER 12

Dick Rents a Room on Mott Street

Going out into the fresh air Dick felt the pangs of hunger. He decided to have a hearty supper at Lovejoy's Hotel instead of at the cheap restaurant he usually went to. He hid his old clothes and his box in an alley near the Astor House and then proceeded to Lovejoy's. Because of Dick's new clothes, he was treated as a respectable customer and a good supper was placed before him.

"I wish I could come here every day," thought Dick. "It seems kind o' nice and 'spectable, compared to the other place. There's a gent at that other table that I've shined boots for more'n once. He don't know me in my new clothes. Guess he don't know his bootblack patronizes the same establishment."

His supper over, Dick went up to the desk paid for his dinner with the five-dollar bill. Receiving his change he went out into the street.

Two questions now arose: How should he spend the evening, and where should he spend the night? Yesterday, with such a sum of money in his possession, he would have answered both questions easily. For the evening, he would have gone to the Old Bowery Theater, and then gone to sleep in any out-of-the-way place he could find. But today he had turned over a new leaf. He wanted to save his money to aid his advancement in the world. So he could not afford the theater. And, with his new clothes, he was unwilling to spend the night out of doors.

So he determined to find a room he could consider as his own, where he could sleep nights, instead of depending on boxes and old wagons for a chance shelter. This would be the first step towards respectability.

He decided that Fifth Avenue was a little out of his price range. So he made his way to Mott Street, near the rough and dangerous Five Points section of the city. Here he stopped in front of a shabby brick lodging-house kept by a Mrs. Mooney. Dick knew her son Tom.

He rang the bell, which sent back a shrill metallic response.

The door was opened by an untidy servant, who looked at him with curiosity. He looked surprisingly well dressed to be ringing Mrs. Mooney's doorbell.

"Well, Queen Victoria," said Dick, "is your missus at home?"

"My name's Bridget," said the girl.

"Oh, indeed!" said Dick. "You looked so much like the queen's picture what she gave me last Christmas in exchange for mine, that I couldn't help calling you by her name."

"Oh, go along wid ye!" said Bridget. "It's makin' fun ye are."

"Bridget!" called a shrill voice from the basement.

"The missus is calling me," said Bridget, hurriedly. "I'll tell her ye want her."

"All right!" said Dick.

The servant descended into the lower regions. In a short time a stout, red-faced woman appeared in her place.

"Well, sir, what's your wish?" she asked.

"Have you got a room to let?" asked Dick.

"Is it for yourself you ask?" questioned the woman, in some surprise.

Dick answered said it was.

"I haven't got any very good rooms vacant. There's a small room on the third floor."

"I'd like to see it," said Dick.

"I don't know as it would be good enough for you," said the woman, with a glance at Dick's clothes.

"I ain't very partic'lar about accommodations," said Dick. "I guess I'll look at it."

Dick followed the landlady up two narrow staircases, uncarpeted and dirty, to the third landing. Here he was shown into a room about ten feet square. It had once been covered with a cheap carpet, but this was now very ragged and looked worse than none. There was a single bed in the corner, covered with a heap of blankets and sheets, rumpled and not very clean. There was a bureau, with the veneer scratched and in some parts stripped off, and a small mirror, eight inches by ten, cracked across the middle. There were also two shabby chairs.

Judging from Dick's appearance, Mrs. Mooney thought he would turn the room down in disgust. But to Dick even this little room seemed comfortable in comparison with a box or an empty wagon.

"Well, what's the rent?" asked Dick.

"I ought to have a dollar a week," said Mrs. Mooney, hesitatingly.

"Say seventy-five cents, and I'll take it," said Dick.

"Every week in advance?"

"Yes."

"Well, as times is hard, and I can't afford to keep it empty, you may have it. When will you come?"

"Tonight," said Dick.

"It ain't lookin' very neat. I don't know as I can fix it up tonight."

"Well, I'll sleep here tonight, and you can fix it up tomorrow."

"I hope you'll excuse the looks. I'm a lone woman, and my help is so lazy I have to look after everything myself. I can't keep things as straight as I want to."

"All right," said Dick.

"Can you pay me the first week in advance?" asked the landlady, cautiously.

Dick took seventy-five cents from his pocket and placed it in her hand.

"What's your business, sir, if I may inquire?" said Mrs. Mooney.

"Oh, I'm professional!" said Dick.

"Indeed!" said the landlady, who did not feel she had learned much by this answer.

"How's Tom?" asked Dick.

"Do you know my Tom?" said Mrs. Mooney in surprise. "He's gone to sea—to Californy. He went last week."

"Did he?" said Dick. "Yes, I knew him."

Mrs. Mooney looked upon her new lodger with increased favor, on finding that he was acquainted with her son.

"I'll bring over my baggage from the Astor House this evening," said Dick in a tone of importance.

"From the Astor House!" repeated Mrs. Mooney, in fresh amazement.

"Yes, I've been stoppin' there a short time with some friends," said Dick.

"Did you say you was purfessional?" she asked.

"Yes, ma'am," said Dick, politely.

"You ain't a—a—" Mrs. Mooney paused, uncertain what to say.

"Oh, no, nothing of the sort," said Dick, promptly. "How could you think so, Mrs. Mooney?"

"No offence, sir," said the landlady, more confused than ever.

"Certainly not," said our hero. "But you must excuse me now, Mrs. Mooney, as I have business of great importance to attend to."

"You'll come round this evening?"

Dick said he would and turned away.

"I wonder what he is!" thought the landlady, following him with her eyes as he crossed the street. "He's got good clothes on, but he don't seem very particular about his room. Well; I've got all my rooms full now. That's one comfort."

Dick felt more comfortable now that he had taken the decisive step of renting a room and paying a week's rent in advance. For seven nights he was sure of a shelter and a bed to sleep in. The thought was a pleasant one to him. Until now, he had seldom known when he rose in the morning where he would sleep that night.

"I must bring my things round," said Dick to himself. "I guess I'll go to bed early tonight. It'll feel kinder good to sleep in a reg'lar bed. Boxes is rather hard to the back and ain't comfortable in case of rain. I wonder what Johnny Nolan would say if he knew I'd got a room of my own."

CHAPTER 13

Micky Maguire

About nine o'clock Dick returned to his new lodgings. He carried with him the clothes that he had worn at the start of the day and his bootblack box. These he put away in the bureau drawers. By the light of a flickering candle he took off his clothes and went to bed. He thought about the events of the day with satisfaction. Soon, his eyes were closed, and he did not awake until half-past six the next morning.

He lifted himself on his elbow and stared around himself in bewilderment.

"Blest if I hadn't forgot where I was," he said to himself. "So this is my room, is it? Well, it seems kind of 'spectable to have a room and a bed to sleep in. I'd orter be able to afford seventy-five cents a week. I've throwed away more money than that in one evenin'. There ain't no reason why I shouldn't live 'spectable. I wish I knowed as much as Frank. Nobody ever cared enough for me before to give me good advice. It was kicks, and cuffs, and swearin' at me all the time. I'd like to show him I can do something."

In the corner of the room was an ancient washstand with a cracked bowl and broken pitcher. Pouring some water from the pitcher into the bowl, he enjoyed the pleasure of washing his face and hands. Having neither comb nor brush, he arranged his combed his hair with his fingers as best he could. He decided he could purchase a comb and brush as soon as possible, if he could get them cheaply.

For the first time in his life Dick owned two suits of clothes. Should he put on the clothes Frank had given him, or resume his old rags? As he looked at the ragged and dirty coat and the patched pants, Dick felt ashamed of them. Yet, if he went to work in his new suit, he was in danger of spoiling it. He put on the old clothes.

"They don't look 'spectable," he decided, looking at himself. So he took them off again and put on the new suit.

"I must try to earn a little more," he thought, "to pay for my room and to buy some new clothes when these is wore out."

He went downstairs and into the street, carrying his blacking-box with him.

Even though Dick had four dollars in his pocket, he went straight to work. He had decided that he wanted to start a savings account at a bank. That way, he would have some money to fall back on in case of an emergency. He had been used to living day-to-day without a penny ahead. But now a vision of respectability floated before his mind.

As if to encourage Dick in his newborn resolution, he got six jobs in the first hour-and-a-half of work that morning. This gave him sixty cents— enough money to buy breakfast and a comb.

His work had made him hungry. He went into a small restaurant and ordered a cup of coffee, a beefsteak, and two rolls. This was a more luxuriant breakfast than he was used to and it cost him twenty-five cents. He set forth from the restaurant alert and ready to find many customers.

The morning being a busy time with the bootblacks, Dick's changed clothing had not as yet attracted the attention of the other bootblacks. But when business slackened a little, that changed.

Among the down town bootblacks was one from Five Points—a stout, freckled-faced boy of fourteen, named Micky Maguire. He was a reckless boy who led a gang of rough followers. He had served two terms at the Blackwell's Island reformatory, but these had done little to improve his conduct.

Micky was proud of his strength and toughness, and he had a jealous hatred of those who wore good clothes and kept their faces clean.

On this particular morning Micky had not had much business. As a result, his temper, never very friendly, was somewhat ruffled. He had had a very meager breakfast—because of the low state of his finances. He was walking along with one of his friends, Limpy Jim, when he spotted Dick in his new suit.

"My eyes!" he exclaimed, in astonishment; "Jim, just look at Ragged Dick. He' s come into a fortune, and turned gentleman. See his new clothes."

"So he has," said Jim. "Where'd he get 'em, I wonder?"

"Hooked 'em, p'raps. Let's go and stir him up a little. We don't want no gentlemen on our beat. So he's puttin' on airs, is he? I'll teach him a lesson."

The two boys walked up to Dick, whose back was turned, and Micky Maguire gave him a smart slap on the shoulder.

Dick turned around quickly.

CHAPTER 14

A Battle and a Victory

"**W**hat's that for?" demanded Dick, turning round to see who had struck him.

"You're gettin' mighty fine!" said Micky Maguire, eyeing Dick's new clothes with a scornful air.

"Well, what if I am?" he retorted. "Does it hurt you any?"

"See him put on airs, Jim," said Micky. "Where'd you get them clo'es?"

"Never mind where I got 'em. Maybe the Prince of Wales gave 'em to me."

"Hear him, now, Jim," said Micky. "Most likely he stole 'em."

"Stealin' ain't in *my* line."

"Do you mean to say *I* steal?" Micky demanded, doubling up his fist and advancing toward Dick.

"I know you've been to Blackwell's Island twice," Dick said. "P'rhaps you was just there on an inspection tour with the Mayor. Or maybe you was a innocent victim of oppression. I ain't a goin' to say."

Micky's freckled face grew red with anger.

"Do you mean to insult me?" he demanded shaking the fist in Dick's face. "Maybe you want a lickin'?"

"I ain't partic'larly anxious to get one," said Dick, coolly. "They don't agree with my constitution which is nat'rally delicate. I'd rather have a good dinner than a lickin' any time."

"You're afraid," sneered Micky. "Isn't he, Jim?"

"In course he is."

"P'rhaps I am," said Dick, composedly, "but it don't trouble me much."

"Do you want to fight?" demanded Micky, encouraged by Dick's quiet manner.

"No, I don't," said Dick. "I ain't fond of fightin'. It's a very poor amusement and very bad for the complexion, 'specially for the eyes and nose, which is apt to turn red, white, and blue."

Micky misunderstood Dick's words. He judged that Dick would be an easy victim. He knew Dick seldom was involved in any street fight. He assumed it was from cowardice rather than from good sense.

He swung his fist at Dick's face but Dick drew back just in time.

Dick dropped his blacking-box and returned Micky's blow and connected. The young bully staggered back and would have fallen, if he had not been propped up by Limpy Jim.

"Go in, Micky!" shouted Jim. Jim was rather a coward but liked to see others fight. "Polish him off, that's a good feller."

Micky was now boiling over with rage and fury. He threw himself at Dick, and tried to knock him to the ground. But Dick stepped aside and tripped up his opponent, stretching him flat on the sidewalk.

"Hit him, Jim!" shouted Micky, furiously.

Limpy Jim was not inclined to obey orders. There was a quiet strength and coolness about Dick that alarmed him. He preferred that Micky should take all the risks of battle.

"Come, Micky," said Dick, quietly, "you'd better give it up. I wouldn't have touched you if you hadn't tried to hit me first. I don't want to fight. It's low business."

"You're afraid of hurtin' your clo'es," said Micky, with a sneer.

"Maybe I am," said Dick.

Micky's answer to this was another attack, as violent as the first. But his fury was in the way. He struck wildly, and Dick had no difficulty in turning the blow aside, so it fell on empty air. Micky's momentum was such that he nearly fell forward headlong.

Recovering himself, Micky saw that Dick was a more formidable opponent than he had supposed. He was considering another, better planned assault. But there was an unexpected interference.

"Look out! A cop!'" said Jim, in a low voice.

Micky turned round and saw a tall policeman heading towards him. He decided this would be a good time to end the fight. He therefore picked up his black-box, hitched up his pants, and walked off, Limpy Jim at his side.

"What's that chap been doing?" asked the policeman Dick.

"He was amusin' himself takin' a swing at me," replied Dick.

"What for?"

"He didn't like it 'cause I go to a different tailor from him."

"Well, it seems to me you *are* dressed pretty smart for a bootblack," said the policeman.

"I wish I wasn't a bootblack," said Dick.

"Never mind, my lad," said the policeman. "It's an honest business. Stick to it till you get something better."

"I mean to," said Dick.

"Do you see that gentleman over there?" asked the officer, pointing to a well-dressed man who was walking on the other side of the street.

"Yes."

"Well, he was once a newsboy."

"And what is he now?"

"He keeps a bookstore and is quite prosperous."

Dick looked at the gentleman with interest, wondering if he would look as respectable when he was a grown man. For the first time, he began to think that he might not polish boots all his life. In seven years he would be a man, and, since his meeting with Frank, he felt that he would like to be a respectable man.

The next morning, after business had slowed down, he went to a bank. He had never been in a bank before. By mistake, he went to the desk where money was paid out.

"Where's your book?" asked the clerk

"I haven't got any."

"Have you any money deposited here?"

"No, sir, I want to leave some here."

"Then go to the next desk."

Dick followed directions, and presented himself before an elderly man with gray hair, who looked at him over the rims of his spectacles.

"I want you to keep that for me," said Dick, awkwardly emptying his money out on the desk. "How much is there?"

"Four dollars plus another dollar in change."

"Have you got an account here?"

"No, sir."

"Of course you can write?"

"Have I got to do any writing?" asked Dick, a little embarrassed.

"We want you to sign your name in this book," and the old gentleman opened a large book containing the names of depositors.

Dick looked at the book with awe.

"I ain't much on writin'," he said.

"Very well; write as well as you can."

Dick took the pen and after a hard effort, wrote DICK HUNTER.

"Dick! That means Richard, I suppose," said the bank officer, who had some difficulty in making out the signature.

"No; Ragged Dick is what folks call me."

"You don't look very ragged."

"No, I've left my rags to home. They might get wore out if I used 'em too much."

"Well, my lad, I'll make out a savings book in the name of Dick Hunter. I hope you will save up your money and deposit more with us."

Dick took his bankbook and gazed on the

entry "Five Dollars" with a new sense of importance. He used to joke about Erie shares, but now,
for the first time, he felt himself a capitalist; on a
small scale, to be sure, but still it was no small
thing for Dick to have five dollars which he could
call his own. He promised himself that he would
deposit every cent he could spare from his earnings.

But Dick knew that he needed more than
money to win a respectable position in the world.
He felt that he was very ignorant. Dick knew he
must study hard and learn to really read and write.
And he dreaded it. But he meant to learn, never-
theless.

When Dick went home that night, he locked
up his bankbook in one of the drawers of the
bureau. He felt more independent than he had
ever felt before in his life.

CHAPTER 15

Dick Finds a Tutor

The next morning Dick was unusually successful. He got several jobs. And even got paid twenty-five cents for one job when the gentleman refused to take his change. This reminded Dick that he had not yet returned the change to Mr. Greyson, the gentleman whose boots he blacked three days earlier.

"What'll he think of me?" Dick said to himself. "I hope he won't think I'm mean enough to keep the money."

He immediately started for 125 Fulton Street where he found Mr. Greyson's name on the door of an office on the second floor.

Dick walked in.

"Is Mr. Greyson in?" he asked of a clerk who sat on a high stool before a desk.

"Not just now. He'll be in soon. Will you wait?"

"Yes," said Dick.

"Very well. Take a seat then."

Dick sat down. He picked up the morning

Tribune, but soon got stuck on a word of four syllables. He put the newspaper back down. But he had not long to wait, for five minutes later Mr. Greyson entered.

"Did you wish to speak to me, my lad?" said he to Dick. He did not recognize him in his new clothes.

"Yes, sir," said Dick. "I owe you some money."

"Indeed!" said Mr. Greyson, pleasantly. "That's an agreeable surprise. So you are a debtor of mine, and not a creditor?"

"I b'lieve that's right," said Dick, drawing fifteen cents from his pocket and placing in Mr. Greyson's hand.

"Fifteen cents!" he said with surprise. "How do you happen to be indebted to me in that amount?"

"You gave me a quarter for shinin' your boots, the other mornin' and couldn't wait for the change. I meant to have brought it before, but I forgot all about it till this mornin'."

"It had quite slipped my mind too. But you don't look like the boy who shined my boots. He wasn't as well dressed as you."

"No," said Dick. "I was dressed for a party, then, but the clo'es was too well ventilated to be comfortable in cold weather."

"You're an honest boy," said Mr. Greyson. "Who taught you to be honest?"

"Nobody," said Dick. "But it's mean to cheat

and steal. I've always knowed that."

"Then you've got ahead of some of our business men. I'd like to help you out. Will you let me?"

"Yes," said Dick. "I want to grow up 'spectable. But I don't know where to go."

"Then I'll tell you. The church I attend is at the corner of Fifth Avenue and Twenty-first Street."

"I've seen it," said Dick.

"I have a class in the Sunday School there. If you'll come next Sunday, I'll take you into my class and do what I can to help you."

"Thank you," said Dick, "but p'rhaps you'll get tired of teaching me. I'm awful ignorant."

"No, my lad," said Mr. Greyson, kindly. "You clearly have some good principles to start with. You have a promising future."

"Well, you're gettin' up in the world," Dick said to himself, as he left the office, "You've got money invested and are goin' to attend church, by special invitation, on Fifth Avenue. I wouldn't be su'prised if you should find cards, when you get home, from the Mayor, requestin' the honor of your company to dinner, along with other distinguished guests."

Dick was in good spirits. He seemed to be emerging into a new atmosphere of respectability.

At six o'clock Dick went into a restaurant on Chatham Street and got a comfortable supper. He had been so successful during the day that, after paying for this, he still had ninety cents left. While he was eating, another boy came in and sat down beside him. Dick recognized him as a boy who three months before had entered the ranks of the boot-blacks, but who, from a natural timidity, had not been able to earn much. He was ill fitted for the rough companionship of the street boys.

"How are you, Fosdick?" said Dick, as the other seated himself.

"Pretty well," said Fosdick. "I suppose you're all right."

"Oh, yes. I've been havin' a bully supper. What are you goin' to have?"

"Some bread and butter."

"Why don't you get a cup o' coffee?"

"Why," said Fosdick, reluctantly, "I haven't got money enough tonight."

"Never mind," said Dick. "I'm in luck today. I'll treat."

"That's kind in you," said Fosdick, gratefully.

Dick ordered a cup of coffee and a plate of beefsteak for his young companion. Fosdick ate with pleasure. When the meal was over, Dick paid for both suppers and the boys went out into the street together.

"Where are you going to sleep tonight, Fosdick?" asked Dick, as they stood on the sidewalk.

"I don't know," said Fosdick, a little sadly. "In some doorway, I expect. But I'm afraid the police will make me move on."

"I'll tell you what," said Dick. "You must go home with me. I guess my bed will hold two."

"Have you got a room?" asked the other, in surprise.

"Yes," said Dick, rather proudly. "I've got a room over in Mott Street. That'll be better than sleepin' in a door-way, won't it?"

"Yes, indeed it will," said Fosdick. "How lucky I was to come across you! I don't like living as I do. When my father was alive I had every comfort."

"That's more'n I ever had," said Dick. "But I'm goin' to try to live comfortable now. Your father's dead?"

"Yes," said Fosdick, sadly. "He was a printer; but he was drowned one dark night from a Fulton ferry-boat. I have no relations in the city and no money, so I had to go to work as quick as I could. But I don't get on very well."

"Didn't you have no brothers nor sisters?" asked Dick.

"No," said Fosdick; "I feel very lonesome without him. There's a man out West somewhere that owes him two thousand dollars. He used to live in the city and father lent him all his money to help him go into business; but he failed, or pretended to, and went off. If father hadn't lost that money he would have left me well off; but no amount of money would have made up his loss to me."

"P'rhaps you'll get the money again, some-time," said Dick. "For now, come round and see what sort of a room I've got." Then a sudden thought came to him. "Can you read and write well?" he asked.

"Yes," said Fosdick. "Father always kept me at school when he was alive, and I stood pretty well in my classes. I was expecting to enter at the City College of New York in a couple of years."

"Then I'll tell you what," said Dick. "I'll make a bargain with you. I can't read much more'n a pig; and my writin' looks like hens' tracks. I don't want to grow up knowin' no more'n a four-year-old boy. If you'll teach me readin' and writin' evenin's, you can sleep in my room every night. That'll be better'n door-steps or old boxes."

"Do you mean it?" said Fosdick, his face lighting up.

"In course," said Dick. "It's fashionable for young gentlemen to have private tutors so why shouldn't I foller the fashion? You'll be my perfessor. Only you must promise not to be too tough on me if my writin' looks like a rail-fence on a bender."

"I'll try not to be too severe," said Fosdick, laughing. "Have you got anything to read out of?"

"No," said Dick. "My extensive and well-selected library was lost overboard in a storm, when I was sailin' from the Sandwich Islands to the Sahara Desert. But I'll buy a paper. That'll do me a long time."

Dick stopped at a paper-stand and bought a copy of a weekly paper, filled with stories, sketches, and poems.

Soon after, they arrived at Mrs. Mooney's. Dick got a lamp from the landlady. He then led the way into his apartment with the proud air of a man of property.

"Well, how do you like it, Fosdick?" he asked.

Fosdick felt it was pleasant to have shelter, so he did not notice that it was untidy and unattractive.

"It looks very comfortable, Dick," he said.

"The bed ain't very large," said Dick; "but I guess we can get along."

"Oh, yes," said Fosdick, cheerfully. "I don't take up much room."

"Then that's all right. There's two chairs, you see, one for you and one for me. In case the mayor comes in to spend the evenin' socially, he can sit on the bed."

The boys seated themselves and five minutes later, under the guidance of his young tutor, Dick had begun his studies.

CHAPTER 16

The First Lesson

Dick's young tutor was well qualified to instruct him. Henry Fosdick had always studied hard when he was in school. His father, being a printer, had been employed in an office where books were printed. He often brought home new books, which Henry was always glad to read. Henry had acquired an amount of general information.

The two boys drew up their chairs to the rickety table and spread out the paper before them.

"Now, Dick," said Fosdick, "before we begin, I must find out how much you already know. Can you read any?"

"Not enough to hurt me," said Dick. "All I know about readin' you could put in a nutshell, and there'd be room left for a small family."

"I suppose you know the alphabet?"

"Yes," said Dick, "I guess I can call all the letters by name."

"But you never learned to read much?"

"No," said Dick; "but I was a newsboy a little

while; so I learned a little, just so's to find out what the news was. Sometimes I didn't read straight and called the wrong news. One mornin' I asked another boy what the paper said, and he told me the King of Africa was dead. I thought it was all right till folks began to laugh."

"Well, Dick, if you'll study well, you won't make such mistakes in the future. Let me find a good piece for you to begin on," said Fosdick, looking over the paper.

"Find an easy one," said Dick, "with words of one story."

Fosdick found a piece that he thought would do. He discovered that Dick had not exaggerated his deficiencies. Words of two syllables he seldom pronounced right, and he was very surprised when he was told how *through* was pronounced.

"Seems to me it's throwin' away letters to use all them," he said.

"How would you spell it?" asked his young teacher.

"T-h-r-u," said Dick.

"Well," Fosdick replied, "there's a good many other words that are spelled with more letters than they need to have. But it's the fashion, and we must follow it."

Dick was quick and had an excellent capacity. Moreover he was not easily discouraged. He had made up his mind he must know more and did not complain of the difficulty of his task.

At the end of an hour and a half the boys

stopped for the evening.

"You're learning fast, Dick," said Fosdick. "At this rate you will soon learn to read well."

"Will I?" asked Dick with an expression of satisfaction. "I'm glad of that. I don't want to be ignorant. I didn't use to care, but I do now. I want to grow up 'spectable."

"So do I, Dick. We will both help each other, and I am sure we can accomplish something."

"So am I," said Dick. "But them hard words make my head ache. I wonder who made 'em all?"

"I don't know. Have you ever seen a dictionary?"

"No, I can't say I have, though I may have seen him in the street without knowin' him."

"A dictionary is a book containing all the words in the language."

"How many are there?"

"I don't rightly know; but I think there are about fifty thousand."

"It's a pretty large family," said Dick. "Have I got to learn 'em all?"

"That will not be necessary. There are a large number you would never use."

"I'm glad of that," said Dick; "for I don't expect to live to be more'n a hundred, and by that time I wouldn't be more'n half through. But all that readin' has made me tired. I think we ought to turn in."

The boys got ready for bed and put out the lamp. Weary with the day's work, the boys soon sank into a deep and peaceful slumber.

They did not awaken till six o'clock the next morning. Before going out Dick spoke to Mrs. Mooney about taking Fosdick as a roommate. She had no objection as long as he paid her twenty-five cents a week extra. Dick agreed and the arrangement was settled.

This over, the two boys went out and took stations near each other. Dick had a better eye for business than Henry, so he got more customers. When two customers arrived at the same time, he sent one to his friend.

At the end of the week both boys found themselves with surplus earnings. Dick had the satisfaction of adding two dollars and a half to his deposits in his savings account, and Fosdick began an account by depositing seventy-five cents.

On Sunday morning Dick remembered his promise to Mr. Greyson to come to the church on Fifth Avenue. Dick now recalled it with some regret. He had never been inside a church and was worried he would not know what to do. But Henry, finding him wavering, urged him to go and offered to go with him. Dick gladly accepted the offer.

Dick dressed himself with great care and gave his shoes a brilliant shine. Having fully completed his preparations, he went down to the street and, with Henry by his side, crossed over to Broadway. They went as far as Union Square and then turned down Fourteenth Street to Fifth Avenue.

A short walk now brought them to the church. They stood outside, watching the fashionably dressed people who were entering. They were feeling a little undecided as to whether they should enter also when Dick felt a light touch on his shoulder.

Turning round, he met the smiling glance of Mr. Greyson.

"So, my young friend, you have kept your promise," he said. "And who have you brought with you?"

"A friend of mine," said Dick. "His name is Henry Fosdick."

"I am glad you have brought him. Follow me, and I will find you seats."

CHAPTER 17

Dick's First Appearance in Society

The boys followed Mr. Greyson into the church. He led them to a pew where Mrs. Greyson and her daughter, Ida, were already seated. They looked pleasantly at the boys as they entered, smiling a welcome to them.

The morning service began. Dick felt rather awkward. He watched the rest of the congregation so that he would know when to stand and when to sit.

He was sitting next to Ida. It was the first time he had ever been near so well dressed a young lady, and he felt bashful. When the hymns were announced, Ida found the place and offered a hymnbook to him. Dick took it awkwardly. Even though he could not read the words, he kept his eyes fixed steadily on the page until the singing stopped.

When the service was over, people began to file slowly out of church. Dick could not help thinking, "Wonder what Johnny Nolan 'ould say if he could see me now!"

"We have our Sunday School in the afternoon,"

said Mr. Greyson. "I suppose you live at some distance from here?"

"In Mott Street, sir," answered Dick.

"That is too far to go and return. Suppose you and your friend have dinner with us. Then we can come back here together in the afternoon."

Dick was as much astonished at this invitation as if he had really been invited by the Mayor to dine with him and the Board of Aldermen. Mr. Greyson was evidently a rich man, and yet he had actually invited two bootblacks to dine with him.

"I guess we'd better go home, sir," said Dick, hesitating.

"I don't think you can have any very pressing engagements," said Mr. Greyson, good-humoredly. He understood the reason for Dick's hesitation. "So I take it for granted that you both accept."

In a few moments, he found himself walking down Fifth Avenue with Ida by his side. Henry Fosdick walked behind them with Mr. and Mrs. Greyson.

"What is your name?" asked Ida, pleasantly.

He almost answered, "Ragged Dick," but he caught himself in time.

"Dick Hunter," he replied.

"Dick!" repeated Ida. "That means Richard, doesn't it?"

"Everybody calls me Dick."

"I like the name of Dick," said the young lady. "I have a cousin named Dick."

Without being able to tell why, Dick felt glad

she did. He asked her name.

"My name is Ida," she answered. "Do you like it?"

"Yes," said Dick. "It's a bully name."

Dick turned red as soon as he had said it, for he felt that he had not used the right expression.

The little girl broke into a silvery laugh.

"What a funny boy you are!" she said.

"I didn't mean it," said Dick, stammering. "I meant it's a tip-top name."

Here Ida laughed again, and Dick wished he were back in Mott Street.

"How old are you?" inquired Ida.

"I'm fourteen—goin' on fifteen," said Dick.

"You're a big boy of your age," said Ida.

"How old be you?" asked Dick, beginning to feel more at ease.

"I'm nine years old," said Ida. "I go to Miss Jarvis's school. I've just begun to learn French. Do you know French?"

"Not enough to hurt me," said Dick.

Ida laughed again.

"Do you like it?" asked Dick.

"I like it pretty well, except the verbs. I can't remember them well. Do you go to school?"

"I'm studying with a private tutor," said Dick.

"Are you? So is my cousin Dick. He's going to college this year. Are you going to college?"

"Not this year."

They turned down Twenty-fourth Street, passing the Fifth Avenue Hotel on the left, and stopped before an elegant house with a brown stone front. The boys followed Mr. Greyson into a handsome hall. They were told where to hang their hats. Then they were led into a comfortable parlor.

Dick took his seat on the edge of a sofa, and was tempted to rub his eyes to make sure that he was really awake. He could hardly believe that he was a guest in so fine a mansion.

"Do you like pictures?" she asked the boys.

"Very much," answered Henry.

The little girl brought a book of handsome engravings and seated herself beside Dick. She then began to show him the pictures in the book.

"There are the Pyramids of Egypt," she said.

"What are they for?" asked Dick, puzzled. "I don't see any winders."

"No," said Ida, "I don't believe anybody lives there. Do they, papa?"

"No, my dear. They were used for the burial of the dead. They are some of the largest buildings in the world."

"Is Egypt near here?" asked Dick.

"Oh, no, it's ever so many miles off; about four or five hundred."

"You don't appear to be very accurate in your information, Ida," said her mother. "Four or five thousand miles would be nearer the truth."

After a little more conversation they sat down to dinner. Dick seated himself in an embarrassed way. He was very much afraid of doing or saying something improper. He had the uncomfortable feeling that everybody was looking at him and watching his behavior.

"Where do you live, Dick?" asked Ida.

"In Mott Street."

"Where is that?"

"More than a mile off."

"Is it a nice street?"

"Not very," said Dick. "Only poor folks live there."

"Are you poor?"

"Little girls should be seen and not heard," said her mother, gently. "Dick cannot be called poor, my child, since he earns his living by his own hard work."

"Do you earn your living?" asked Ida. "What do you do?"

Dick blushed. At such a table, and in presence of the servant who was standing at that moment behind his chair, he did not like to say that he was a bootblack.

Mr. Greyson sensed Dick's discomfort and said, "You are too full of questions, Ida. Sometime Dick may tell you, but you know we don't talk of business on Sundays."

Dick in his embarrassment had swallowed a large spoonful of hot soup and almost choked. In spite of the prospect of the best dinner he had ever eaten, he wished he were back in Mott Street.

Although Dick was ill at ease, he got along pretty well at the table by noticing how the others acted.

At length they arose from the table, to Dick's

relief. When the boys were about to leave the house with Mr. Greyson for the Sunday School, Ida placed her hand in Dick's, and said, "You'll come again, Dick, won't you?"

"Thank you," said Dick, "I'd like to." He could not help thinking Ida the nicest girl he had ever seen.

"Yes," said Mrs. Greyson, "we will be glad to see you both here again."

"Thank you very much," said Henry. "We would like very much to come."

In the Sunday School class, Dick had not heard the stories they talked about. He found them interesting and, when the class was over, promised to come again the next Sunday.

As Dick and Henry walked toward Mott Street, Dick could not help thinking about the sweet little girl who had welcomed him so warmly. He hoped he might meet her again.

"Mr. Greyson is a nice man, isn't he, Dick?" asked Henry, as they were turning into Mott Street.

"Ain't he, though?" said Dick. "He treated us just as if we were young gentlemen."

"Ida seemed to take a liking to you."

"She's a tip-top girl," said Dick, "but she asked so many questions that I didn't know what to say."

He had barely finished speaking when a stone whizzed by his head. Turning quickly, he saw Micky Maguire running round the corner of the street they had just passed.

CHAPTER 18

Micky Maguire's Second Defeat

Dick was no coward. When he saw that Micky had thrown the stone, he instantly turned and gave chase. Micky ran as fast as he could. But just as he entered a narrow alley, he tripped and fell on the hard stones. He was on the ground when Dick caught up.

"Ow!" he whined. "Don't you hit a feller when he's down."

"Why did you throw that stone at me?" demanded Dick, looking down at the fallen bully.

"Just for fun," said Micky.

"S'posin' I fire a rock at you jest for fun," Dick said.

"Don't!" exclaimed Micky, in alarm.

"You don't think that sounds like fun?" Dick asked.

"I've nearly broke my arm," said Micky, rubbing the affected limb.

"If it's broke you can't fire no more stones, which is a very cheerin' thought," said Dick. "If you haven't money enough to buy a wooden one I'll lend you a quarter. There's one good thing about wooden ones, they ain't liable to get cold in winter, which is another cheerin' thought."

"I don't want none of yer cheerin' thoughts," said Micky, sullenly. "Yer company ain't wanted here."

"Thank you for your polite invitation to leave," said Dick, bowing. "I'm willin' to go, but if you throw any more stones at me, Micky Maguire, I'll hurt you worse than your fall did."

Micky scowled but said nothing.

"As I've got a friend waitin', I shall have to tear myself away," said Dick. "You'd better not throw any more stones, Micky Maguire, for it's bad for your health."

Micky muttered something which Dick did not stay to hear. He backed out of the alley, keeping a watchful eye on his fallen foe.

"Who was it, Dick?" Henry asked when Dick rejoined him.

"A partic'lar friend of mine, Micky Maguire," said Dick. "He playfully fired a rock at my head as a mark of his affection. He loves me like a brother, Micky does."

"Rather a dangerous kind of a friend, I should think," said Fosdick.

"I've warned him not to be so affectionate another time," said Dick.

"I know him," said Henry Fosdick. "He's the head of a gang from Five-Points. He threatened to beat me once because a gentleman asked me to black his boots instead of him."

"He's been at Blackwell's Island two or three times for stealing," said Dick. "I guess he won't touch me again. He'd rather get hold of small boys. If he ever does anything to you, Fosdick, just let me know, and I'll give him a thrashing."

Over the next few weeks, life went smoothly for Dick and Henry. Dick spent two hours every evening studying with Henry. His progress was astonishingly rapid. They were a good combination for Dick was a quick and enthusiastic student and Henry was a good teacher.

"You're improving wonderfully, Dick," said his friend, one evening, when Dick had read an entire paragraph without a mistake.

"Am I?" said Dick.

"Yes. If you'll buy a writing-book tomorrow, we can begin writing tomorrow evening."

"What else do you know, Henry?"

"Arithmetic, and geography, and grammar."

"You know a lot!" said Dick, admiringly.

"I don't *know* any of them," said Fosdick. "I've only studied them. I wish I knew a great deal more."

"I'll be satisfied when I know as much as you," said Dick.

"It seems a great deal to you now, Dick, but in a few months you'll think differently. The more you know, the more you'll want to know."

"Then there ain't any end to learnin'?" said Dick.

"No."

"Well," said Dick, "I guess I'll be as much as sixty before I know everything. Anyway, you know too much to be blackin' boots. Leave that to ignorant chaps like me."

"You won't be ignorant long, Dick."

"You'd ought to get a job in some office as a

messenger or a clerk."

"I wish I could," said Fosdick, earnestly. "I've thought of trying to get a place, but no one would take me with these clothes." He glanced at his well-worn suit. He kept as neat as he could, but if had begun to show decided marks of use.

"I almost wanted to stay at home from Sunday School last Sunday," he continued, "because I thought everybody would notice how dirty and worn my clothes had got to be."

"If my clothes wasn't two sizes too big for you," said Dick, generously, "I'd change."

"That's very kind," said Fosdick. "Your suit is much better than mine. But I'd look like I was swimming in it."

"I say," Dick said with a sudden thought, "how much money have we got in the bank?"

Fosdick took a key from his pocket, and went to the drawer where the bankbooks were kept.

Dick had eighteen dollars and ninety cents placed to his credit, while Fosdick had six dollars and forty-five cents.

"How much does that make all together?" asked Dick.

"It makes twenty-five dollars and thirty-five cents, Dick," said Henry.

"Take it, and buy some clothes, Henry," said Dick.

"What, your money too?"

"Of course."

"No, Dick, I couldn't think of it. Almost

three-quarters of the money is yours."

"I don't need it," said Dick.

"You may not need it now, but you will some time."

"I'll have some more by then."

"That may be; but it wouldn't be fair for me to use your money, Dick."

"Well, I'll lend it to you, then," persisted Dick, "and you can pay me when you get to be a rich merchant."

Finally, after much urging by Dick, Henry agreed to use whatever of the money he needed to get a suit.

The next day they withdrew the money from the bank. In the afternoon, when business slacked off, they set out in search of a clothing store. Dick knew enough of the city to be able to find a place where they could get a bargain. He was determined that Fosdick should have a good suit, even if it took all the money they had. The result of their search was that for twenty-three dollars Fosdick got a complete outfit, including a couple of shirts, a hat, and a pair of shoes.

When they arrived back at their room on Mott Street, Fosdick at once tried on his new suit. It was an excellent fit. Dick looked at his friend with satisfaction.

"You look like a young gentleman of fortune," he said, "and do credit to your governor."

"I suppose that means you, Dick," said Fosdick, laughing.

"Of course it does," said Dick, with mock seriousness. "And if you don't show your gov'nor the proper respect, I'll cut you off without a penny, you young dog!"

Then they both laughed.

CHAPTER 19

Fosdick Changes His Business

Fosdick did not wear his new clothes while shining shoes. Instead, about ten o' clock in the morning, when business slackened, he went home and changed. Then he went to a hotel where he could see copies of the *Morning Herald* and the *Sun*. Noting down the businesses that were advertising a job for a boy, he then went on a round of applications.

But he found it no easy thing to get a place. Swarms of boys seemed to be out of work. It was not unusual to find from fifty to a hundred applicants for a single position.

After fifty applications and as many failures, Fosdick began to get discouraged. There seemed to be no way out of his present business, for which he felt unfitted.

"I may have to black boots all my life," he said one day to Dick.

"Keep a stiff upper lip," said Dick. "By the time you get to be a gray-headed veteran, you may get a chance to run errands for some big firm on the Bowery. That is a very cheerin' thought."

Dick's jokes and perpetual good spirits kept up Fosdick's courage.

"As for me," said Dick, "I expect by that time to lay up a colossal fortun' out of shines, and live in princely style on the Avenue."

One morning, straying into French's Hotel, Fosdick discovered the following advertisement in the columns of *The Herald:*

> **WANTED—A smart, capable boy to run errands, and make himself generally useful in a hat and cap store. Salary three dollars a week at first. Inquire at No. __ Broadway, after ten o'clock, A.M.**

It was just ten o'clock, so he lost no time in making his way to the store. It was easy to find the store, as nearly twenty boys were already assembled in front of it. They eyed one another cautiously, feeling that they were rivals, and mentally calculating each other's chances.

"There isn't much chance for me," said Fosdick to Dick, who had accompanied him. "Look at all these boys. Most of them have good homes, I suppose, and good recommendations, while I have neither of those."

"Go ahead," said Dick. "Your chance is as good as anybody's."

At this moment, one of the boys, a rather proud-looking young gentleman, suddenly turned to Dick, and remarked, "I've seen you before."

"Oh, have you?" said Dick, whirling round; "then p'rhaps you'd like to see me behind."

At this unexpected answer all the other boys burst into a laugh.

"I've seen you somewhere," he said, in a surly tone, correcting himself.

"Most likely you have," said Dick. "That's where I generally keep myself."

There was another laugh at the expense of Roswell Crawford, for that was the name of the young aristocrat. But he had his revenge ready. He said, "I know you for all your impudence. You're nothing but a bootblack."

This information took the boys who were standing around by surprise, for Dick was well dressed, and was not carrying his box and brush.

"S'pose I be," said Dick. "Have you got any objection?"

"Not at all," said Roswell, curling his lip; "only you'd better stick to blacking boots and not try to get into a store."

"Thank you for your kind advice," said Dick. "Is it gratuitous, or do you expect to be paid for it?"

"You're an impudent fellow."

"That's a very cheerin' thought," said Dick, good-naturedly.

"Do you expect to get this place when there's gentlemen's sons applying for it? A bootblack in a store! That would be a good joke."

"Don't trouble yourself," said Dick. "I ain't

agoin' to cut you out. I can't afford to give up a independent and lucrative purfession for a salary of three dollars a week."

"Hear him talk!" said Roswell Crawford, with an unpleasant sneer. "If you are not trying to get the place, what are you here for?"

"I came with a friend of mine," said Dick, indicating Fosdick, "who is applying for the position."

"Is he a bootblack, too?" demanded Roswell.

"He!" replied Dick. "Didn't you know his father was a member of Congress, and intimately acquainted with all the biggest men in the State?"

The boys looked Fosdick as if they did not know whether to believe this statement or not. Just then the owner of the store, Mr. Henderson, came to the door. Casting his eyes over the waiting group, he singled out Roswell Crawford and asked him to enter.

"Well, my lad, how old are you?"

"Fourteen years old," said Roswell.

"Are your parents living?"

"Only my mother. My father is dead. He was a gentleman," he added.

"Oh, was he?" said the shopkeeper. "Do you live in the city?"

"Yes, sir. In Clinton Place."

"Have you ever had a job before?"

"Yes, sir," said Roswell, a little reluctantly.

"Where was it?"

"In an office on Dey Street."

"How long were you there?"

"A week."

"It seems to me that was a short time. Why did you not stay longer?"

"Because," said Roswell, "the man wanted me to get to the office at eight o'clock, and make the fire. I'm a gentleman's son and am not used to such dirty work."

"Indeed!" said the shopkeeper. "Well, young gentleman, you may step aside a few minutes. I will speak with some of the other boys before making my selection."

Several other boys were called in and questioned. Roswell stood by and listened with an air of self-satisfaction. "The man can see I'm a gentleman and will do credit to his store," he thought to himself.

Eventually it came to Fosdick's turn. He was not optimistic about his chances. Unlike Roswell, he had a very low estimate of his qualifications when compared with those of other applicants. But his quiet, gentlemanly manner appealed to the shopkeeper.

"Do you reside in the city?" he asked.

"Yes, sir," said Henry.

"What is your age?"

"Twelve."

"Have you ever had a position?"

"No, sir."

"I would like to see a sample of your handwriting. Here, take the pen and write your name."

Henry Fosdick had a very handsome handwriting for a boy of his age, while Roswell, who had submitted to the same test, could do little more than scrawl.

"Do you live with your parents?"

"No, sir, they are dead."

"Where do you live, then?"

"In Mott Street."

Roswell curled his lip when this name was pronounced.

"Have you any recommendations?" asked Mr. Henderson.

Fosdick hesitated. This was the question he knew would give him trouble.

But at this moment it happened that Mr. Greyson entered the shop with the intention of buying a hat.

"Yes," said Fosdick, promptly. "I will refer to this gentleman."

"How do you do, Fosdick?" asked Mr. Greyson, noticing him for the first time. "How do you happen to be here?"

"I am applying for a place, sir," said Fosdick. "May I refer the gentleman to you?"

"Certainly, I will be glad to speak a good word for you. Mr. Henderson, this is a member of my Sunday-school class, of whose good qualities and good abilities I can speak confidently."

"That will be sufficient," said Mr. Henderson. "He could have no better recommendation than your recommendation, Mr. Greyson. Young man, you may come to the store tomorrow morning at half past seven o'clock. The pay will be three dollars a week for the first six months. If I am satisfied with you, I will then raise it to five dollars."

The other boys looked disappointed, but none more so than Roswell Crawford. He would have cared less if any one else had gotten the job; but for a boy who lived in Mott Street to be preferred to him, a gentleman's son, he considered indeed humiliating. In a spirit of petty spite, he said, "He's a bootblack. Ask him if he isn't."

"He's an honest and intelligent lad," said Mr. Greyson. "As for you, young man, I only hope you have one-half his good qualities."

Roswell Crawford left the store in disgust, and the other unsuccessful applicants with him.

"What luck, Fosdick?" asked Dick, as his friend came out of the store.

"I've got the place," said Fosdick. "But it was only because Mr. Greyson spoke up for me."

Both Dick and Henry were pleased at the success of the application. The pay would be small. But, if he planned carefully, Fosdick thought he could get along on it. Dick decided, as soon as his education would permit, to follow his companion's example.

"I don't know as you'll be willin' to room with a bootblack," he said, to Henry, "now you're goin' into business."

"I couldn't room with a better friend, Dick," said Fosdick. "When we part, it'll be because you wish it."

So Fosdick entered on a new career.

CHAPTER 20

Nine Months Later

Nine months later, Fosdick was still at the hat-store. His wages had been raised to five dollars a week. He and Dick still had their room at Mrs. Mooney's lodging-house, and lived very frugally, so that both were able to save up money. Dick had been unusually successful in business. He had several regular patrons. From two of them he had received presents of clothing, which had saved him expense on that score. His income had averaged almost seven dollars a week. Of this amount he continued to pay one dollar weekly for the room, but he was still able to save one half the remainder. He had now accumulated one hundred and seventeen dollars in his savings account.

"You'll be a rich man some time, Dick," said Henry Fosdick, one evening.

"And live on Fifth Avenue," said Dick.

"Perhaps so. Stranger things have happened."

"Well," said Dick, "when you see a Fifth

Avenue mansion for sale for a hundred and seventeen dollars, just let me know and I'll buy it as an investment."

But, over the nine months, Dick had gained something more valuable than money. He had studied regularly every evening, and his improvement had been marvelous. He could now read well, write a fair hand, and had studied arithmetic. Besides this he had learned some grammar and geography

"Dick," said Fosdick, one evening, after they had completed their studies, "I think you'll have to get another teacher soon."

"Why?" asked Dick, in some surprise. "Have you been offered a more lucrative position?"

"No," said Fosdick, "but I have taught you all I know myself. You are now as good a scholar as I am."

"Is that true?" said Dick, eagerly.

"Yes," said Fosdick. "You've made wonderful progress. I propose, now that evening schools are in session, that we join one, and study together through the winter."

"All right," said Dick. "I'd be willin' to go now. But do you really mean, Fosdick, that I know as much as you?"

"Yes, Dick, it's true."

"Then I've got you to thank for it," said Dick, earnestly.

"And haven't you paid me, Dick?"

"By payin' the room rent?" said Dick. "What's that? It isn't half enough. I wish you'd take half my money; you deserve it."

"Thank you, Dick, but you're too generous. You've more than paid me. Who gave me money to buy clothes, and so got me my position?"

"Oh, that's nothing!" said Dick.

"It's a great deal, Dick. I will never forget it. But now it seems to me you might try to get a situation yourself."

"Do I know enough?"

"You know as much as I do."

"Then I'll try," said Dick, decidedly.

"I wish there was a place in our store," said Fosdick.

"Never mind," said Dick. "There'll be plenty of other chances. P'rhaps A. T. Stewart might like a partner. I wouldn't ask more'n a quarter of the profits."

"Which would be a very reasonable request on your part," said Fosdick, smiling. "But perhaps Mr. Stewart might object to a partner living on Mott Street."

"I'd be glad to leave Mott Street," said Dick.

"You know," said Fosdick, "I have been thinking it might be a good plan for us to move when we could afford to. Mrs. Mooney doesn't keep the room quite so neat as she might."

"No," said Dick. "She ain't got no prejudices against dirt."

"Yes," said Fosdick, "I've got about tired of it. I guess we can find some better place without having to pay much more. When we move, you must let me pay my share of the rent."

"We'll see about that," said Dick. "Do you propose to move to Fifth Avenue?"

"Not just at the moment, but to some more agreeable neighborhood than this. We'll wait till you get a situation, and then we can decide."

A few days later, as Dick was looking about for customers in the neighborhood of the Park, his attention was drawn to a fellow bootblack. It was a boy about a year younger than himself. He appeared to have been crying.

"What's the matter, Tom?" asked Dick. "Haven't you had luck today?"

"Pretty good," said the boy. "But we're havin' hard times at home. Mother fell last week and broke her arm, and tomorrow we've got to pay the rent, and if we don't the landlord says he'll turn us out."

"Haven't you got anything except what you earn?" asked Dick.

"No," said Tom, "not now. Mother used to earn three or four dollars a week; but she can't do nothin' now, and my little sister and brother are too young."

Dick knew that Tom Wilkins was an excellent boy who never wasted his money.

"I'm sorry for you, Tom," he said. "How much do you owe for rent?"

"Two weeks now," said Tom.

"How much is it a week?"

"Two dollars a week—that makes four."

"Have you got anything towards it?"

"No; I've had to spend all my money for food for mother and the rest of us. I've had pretty hard work to do that. I don't know what we'll do. We haven't any place to go to."

"Can't you borrow the money somewhere?" asked Dick.

Tom shook his head glumly.

"All the people I know are as poor as I am," he said. "They'd help me if they could, but it's hard work for them to get along themselves."

"I'll tell you what, Tom," said Dick, "I'll help you out."

"Have you got any money?" asked Tom, doubtfully.

"Got any money!" repeated Dick. "Don't you know that I run a bank on my own account? How much is it you need?"

"Four dollars," said Tom. "If we don't pay that before tomorrow night, out we go. You haven't got as much as that, have you?"

"Here are three dollars," said Dick, drawing out his wallet. "I'll let you have the rest tomorrow, and maybe a little more."

"You're a good friend, Dick," said Tom. "But won't you want it yourself?"

"Oh, I've got some more," said Dick.

"Maybe I'll never be able to pay you."

"S'pose you don't," said Dick; "I guess I won't fail."

"I won't forget it, Dick. I hope I'll be able to do somethin' for you sometime."

"All right," said Dick. "I'd ought to help you. I haven't got no mother to look out for. I wish I had."

Dick began to whistle as he turned away, only adding, "I'll see you tomorrow, Tom."

The three dollars that Dick had handed to

Tom Wilkins were his savings for the week. It was now Thursday afternoon. He expected to save the rent out of the earnings of Friday and Saturday. In order to give Tom the additional money he had promised, Dick would have to take it out of his bank savings. He would not have touched that money for any other reason but this. But he felt that it would be selfish to allow Tom and his mother to suffer when he had it in his power to help them.

CHAPTER 21

Dick Loses His Bankbook

Having told Tom Wilkins he would give him more money tomorrow, Dick went to the drawer where he and Fosdick kept their bankbooks. To his surprise the drawer was empty.

"Come here a minute, Fosdick," he said.

"What's the matter, Dick?"

"I can't find my bankbook, nor yours either. What's come of them?"

"I took mine with me this morning, thinking I might want to put in a little more money. I've got it in my pocket."

"But where's mine?" asked Dick.

"I don't know. I saw it in the drawer when I took mine this morning."

"Did you lock the drawer again?" asked Dick.

"Yes. Didn't you have to unlock it just now?"

"So I did," said Dick. "But the drawer is empty now. Somebody opened it with a key and then locked it again."

"Don't give it up, Dick. You haven't lost the money, only the bankbook."

"Ain't that the same thing?"

"No. You can go to the bank tomorrow morning, as soon as it opens, and tell them you have lost the book, and ask them not to pay the money to any one except yourself."

"So I can," said Dick, brightening up. "That is, if the thief hasn't been to the bank today."

"If he has, they might detect him by his handwriting."

"I'd like to get hold of the one that stole it," said Dick. "I'd teach him a lesson."

"It must have been somebody in the house. Suppose we go and see Mrs. Mooney. She may know whether anybody came into our room today."

The two boys went downstairs and knocked at the door of a little back sitting room where Mrs. Mooney generally spent her evenings. It was a shabby little room, with a threadbare carpet on the floor. Mrs. Mooney was seated beside a small pine worktable, industriously mending stockings.

"Good-evening, Mrs. Mooney," said Fosdick.

"Good-evening," said the landlady. "Sit down, if you can find chairs."

"We can't stay long, Mrs. Mooney, but my friend here has had something taken from his room today, and we thought we'd come and see you about it."

"What is it?" asked the landlady. "You don't

think I'd take anything? I'm a poor widow, but I am honest. All my lodgers will tell you that."

"Of course we don't think you took it, Mrs. Mooney. But there are others in the house that may not be honest. My friend has lost his bankbook. It was safe in the drawer this morning, but tonight it is gone."

"How much money was there in the account?" asked Mrs. Mooney.

"Over a hundred dollars," said Fosdick.

"It was my whole fortune," said Dick. "I was goin' to buy a house next year."

"Was the drawer locked?" she asked.

"Yes."

"Then it couldn't have been Bridget. I don't think she has any keys."

"She wouldn't know what a bankbook was," said Fosdick. "You didn't see any of the lodgers go into our room today, did you?"

"I shouldn't wonder if it was Jim Travis," said Mrs. Mooney.

James Travis was a bartender in a run-down bar on Mulberry Street. He was a coarse-looking fellow who looked as if he drank a good bit himself. He occupied a room opposite Dick's. The two boys often heard him reeling upstairs in a state of drunkenness, muttering oaths to himself.

Several times Travis had invited the boys to stop by the bar where he worked and have a drink. But the boys had never accepted the invitation. Neither of them found anything particularly charming about him. The rejection of his invitations had caused Travis to take a dislike to Dick and Henry. He considered them stiff and unsocial.

"What makes you think it was Travis?" asked Fosdick. "He isn't at home in the daytime."

"But he was today. He said he had got a bad cold and had to come home for a clean handkerchief."

"Did you see him?" asked Dick.

"Yes," said Mrs. Mooney. "Bridget was hanging out clothes, and I went to the door to let him in."

"I wonder if he had a key that would fit our drawer," said Fosdick.

"Yes," said Mrs. Mooney. "The bureaus in the two rooms are just alike. I got 'em at auction, and most likely the locks is the same."

"He must be the one," said Dick. "But what's to be done? Of course he'll say he hasn't got it. And he won't be such a fool as to leave it in his room."

"If he hasn't been to the bank, it's all right," said Fosdick. "You can go there the first thing tomorrow morning and stop their paying any money on it."

"But I can't get any money on it myself," said Dick. "I told Tom Wilkins I'd let him have some more money tomorrow, or his sick mother'll put out on the street."

"How much money were you going to give him?"

"I gave him three dollars today and was goin' to give him two dollars tomorrow."

"I've got the money, Dick. I didn't go to the bank this morning."

"All right. I'll pay you back next week. But I hope Jim Travis hasn't emptied my bank account. I thought I was rich this morning, but now I'm in bad circumstances."

"Cheer up, Dick; you'll get your money back."

"I hope so," said Dick, somewhat glumly.

Dick was beginning to feel the bitterness of a reverse of circumstances. With more than one hundred dollars carefully laid away in the savings bank, he had felt quite independent. He was beginning to feel the advantages of his steady self-denial and to experience the pleasures of property. Even more important, he had found great satisfaction at being able to use his money to help Tom Wilkins in his trouble.

Besides this, there was another thought that troubled him. When he got a job in a shop or an office he could not expect to receive as much as he was now making from blacking boots. He had assumed he would be able to use his savings to carry him along for the first year or so. If he did not recover his money, he would have to continue polishing shoes for at least six months longer. This was a discouraging thought.

The two boys discussed whether or not to bring the matter up with Travis. Fosdick was opposed to it.

"It will only put him on his guard," he said, "and I don't see as it will do any good. Of course he will deny it. We'd better keep quiet and watch him. By giving notice at the bank, we can make sure that he doesn't get your money. If he does show up at the bank, they will know at once that he is a thief, and he can be arrested."

This view seemed reasonable. Dick began to think prospects were brighter than he had at first supposed, and his spirits rose a little.

The boys were just on the point of going to bed when there was a knock at the door. To their surprise, it was Jim Travis. He was a pale-faced young man with dark hair and bloodshot eyes. He darted a quick glance at each boy as he entered.

"How are ye, tonight?" he said, sinking into one of the two chairs.

"Jolly," said Dick. "How are you?"

"Tired as a dog," he replied. "Hard work and poor pay. That's the way with me."

Here he darted another quick glance at the boys.

"You don't go out much, do you?" he said.

"Not much," said Fosdick. "We spend our evenings in study."

"That's a waste," said Travis, rather contemptuously. "What's the use of studying so much? You don't expect to be a lawyer, do you, or anything of that sort?"

"Maybe," said Dick. "I haven't made up my mind yet. Whatever I decide to do, readin' and writin' might come handy."

"Well," said Travis, rather abruptly, "I'm tired and I guess I'll turn in."

"Good-night," said Fosdick.

The boys looked at each other as their visitor left the room.

"He came in to see if we'd missed the bank-book," said Dick.

"And to turn off suspicion from himself by letting us know he had no money," added Fosdick.

"That's so," said Dick. "I'd like to have searched them pockets of his."

CHAPTER 22

Tracking the Thief

Jim Travis, like many young men, was able to spend more money than he was able to earn. In addition, he had no great fancy for work at all and would have been glad to find some other way of obtaining money enough to live on. He had recently received a letter from an old companion who had strayed out to California and gotten possession of a claim to a gold mine. He wrote to Travis that he had already made two thousand dollars from it and expected to make his fortune within six months.

Two thousand dollars! Travis was at once inflamed with the desire to go out to California and try his luck. In his present situation he only received thirty dollars a month, but that went a very little way towards gratifying his expensive tastes. He decided to take the next steamer to the land of gold, if he could possibly manage to get money enough to pay the passage.

The price of passage was seventy-five dollars.

Travis's available funds consisted of two dollars and a quarter. Travis asked to two or three of his companions for help. One of these friends offered to lend him thirty-seven cents and another a dollar. But neither of these offers was very encouraging. He was about giving up his project when he happened to overhear Dick discussing his savings with Fosdick.

One hundred and seventeen dollars! Why, that would not only pay his passage but carry him up to the mines after he had arrived in San Francisco. Knowing that neither of the boys were in their room in the daytime, he came back in the course of the morning. When Mrs. Mooney opened the front door, he told her that he had a cold and had come back for a handkerchief. The landlady suspected nothing, and, returning at once to her work in the kitchen, left the coast clear.

Travis at once entered Dick's room and tried the bureau drawers. One of them was locked. He concluded that it must contain Dick's savings. He went back to his own room and got the key from his own bureau. He was pleased to find that it opened the lock on Dick's drawer.

When he discovered the bankbook, his joy was mingled with disappointment. He had expected to find cash. Obtaining money at the savings bank would involve fresh risk. Travis hesitated whether to take it or not but finally decided that it would be worth the trouble. He slipped the book into his pocket, locked the drawer again, and went downstairs and into the street.

There would have been time to go to the savings bank that day, but Travis had already been absent from the bar for some time, so he decided he should not to take the time to go to the savings bank that day. Besides, never having been in a savings bank, he thought it would wise to look over the rules and regulations and see if he could get some information as to how he ought to proceed.

In the evening, it occurred to Travis to find out whether Dick had discovered his loss. When he visited Dick and Henry in their room, he was misled by the boys' silence on the subject. He concluded that nothing had yet been discovered.

"Good!" thought Travis, with satisfaction. "If they don't find out for twenty-four hours, it'll be too late."

Realizing that the boys might discover the loss in the morning, Travis decided he should try to find out. In the morning he waited until he heard the boys come out and then opened his own door.

"Morning, gents," said he sociably. "Going to business?"

"Yes," said Dick. "I'm afraid my clerks'll be lazy if I ain't on hand."

"Good joke!" said Travis. "If you pay good wages, I'll come work for you."

"I pay all I get myself," said Dick. "How's business with you?"

"So-so. Why don't you call round, some time?"

"All my evenin's is devoted to literatoor and science," said Dick. "Thank you all the same."

"By the by, you haven't any of you gents seen a pearl-handled knife, have you?" Travis asked.

"No," said Fosdick. "Have you lost one?"

"Yes," lied Travis. "I left it on my bureau a day or two ago. I've missed one or two other little matters. Bridget don't look to me any too honest. Likely she's got 'em."

"What are you goin' to do about it?" said Dick.

"I'll keep mum unless I lose something more, and then I'll kick up a fuss and haul her over the coals. Have you missed anything?"

"No," said Fosdick, answering for himself.

There was a gleam of satisfaction in the eyes of Travis as he heard this. "They haven't found it out yet," he thought. "I'll bag the money today, and they'll be out of luck."

Having gotten his information, he said good-bye to them and turned down another street.

"He's mighty friendly all of a sudden," said Dick.

"Yes," said Fosdick. "We've put him on the wrong track. He means to get his money today, no doubt. Of course, Dick, you'll be on hand as soon as the bank opens."

"Of course. Jim Travis'll find he's walked into the wrong shop."

"The bank opens at ten o'clock, you know."

"I'll be there on time."

"Good luck, Dick," said Fosdick, as he parted

from him. "It'll all come out right, I think."

"I hope it will," said Dick.

The bank would not open for another two hours and a half. This was the time of day when Dick was the busiest and he didn't want to lose the opportunity. He succeeded in getting six customers, which earned him sixty cents. He then went to a restaurant and got some breakfast. It was now half-past nine. Dick left his box with Johnny Nolan and made his way to the bank.

The officers had not yet arrived, and Dick waited outside for the bank to open. He was a little uneasy, fearing that Travis might be as prompt as himself and, finding him there, might suspect something and so escape the snare. But, looking cautiously up and down the street, he could discover no traces of the thief. When the clock struck ten, the doors of the bank were thrown open, and Dick entered.

As Dick had been made a deposit every week for the last nine months, the cashier knew him by sight.

"You're early, this morning, my lad," he said, pleasantly. "Have you got some more money to deposit? You'll be getting rich, soon."

"I don't know about that," said Dick. "My bankbook's been stole."

"Stolen!" echoed the cashier. "That's unfortunate. Not so bad as it might be, though. The thief can't collect the money."

"That's what I came to see about," said Dick.

"I was afraid he might have got it already."

"He hasn't been here yet. Even if he had, I remember you and would have been suspicious of him. When was it taken?"

"Yesterday," said Dick. "I missed it in the evenin' when I got home."

"Have you any suspicion as to the person who took it?" asked the cashier.

Dick told all he knew of the character and suspicious conduct of Jim Travis, and the cashier agreed that Travis was probably the thief. Dick also explained that he thought Travis would visit the bank that morning.

"Very good," said the cashier. "We'll be ready for him. What is the number of your book?"

"No. 5678," said Dick. He then gave the cashier a description of Travis.

"I think I will know him," said the cashier. "He will receive no money from your account."

"Thank you," said Dick.

Feeling relieved, Dick turned towards the door, planning to look for more customers. He had just reached the doors when he saw James Travis crossing the street and coming towards the bank.

"Here he is," he exclaimed, hurrying back. "Can you hide me somewhere? I don't want to be seen."

The cashier understood the situation at once. He quickly opened a little door, and admitted Dick behind the counter.

"Stoop down," he said, "so as not to be seen."

Dick had hardly done so when Jim Travis opened the outer door, and, looking about him in a little uncertainty, walked up to the cashier's desk.

CHAPTER 23

Travis Is Arrested

Jim Travis advanced into the bank with a doubtful step. After a little hesitation, he approached the teller, and, holding out the bankbook, said, "I want to get my money out."

The bank-officer took the book. After looking at it a moment, he said, "How much do you want?"

"The whole of it," said Travis.

"You can draw out any part of it, but to draw out the whole requires a week's notice."

"Then I'll take a hundred dollars."

"Are you the person to whom the book belongs?"

"Yes, sir," said Travis, without hesitation.

"Your name is—"

"Hunter."

The bank clerk went to a file that listed the names of depositors. While he was looking through it, he managed to send another cashier for a policeman. Travis did not notice. Not being used to savings banks, he supposed the delay was normal. After a search, the cashier came back. He handed a piece of paper to Travis and said, "It will be necessary for you to write an order for the money."

Travis took a pen from the ledge and wrote the order, signing his name "Dick Hunter," the name on the outside of the book.

"Your name is Dick Hunter, then?" said the cashier, taking the paper and looking at the thief over his spectacles.

"Yes," said Travis.

"But," continued the cashier, "I find Hunter's age is put down on the bankbook as fourteen. Surely you must be more than that."

Travis began to feel uneasy. At twenty-three, he knew there was no way the cashier would believe he was fourteen.

"Dick Hunter's my younger brother," he said. "I'm getting out the money for him."

"I thought you said your own name was Dick Hunter," said the cashier.

"I said my name was Hunter," said Travis. "I didn't understand you."

"But you've signed the name of Dick Hunter to this order. How is that?" questioned the troublesome cashier.

Travis saw that he was getting himself into a tight place.

"I thought I had to give my brother's name," he answered.

"What is your own name?"

"Henry Hunter."

"Can you bring any one to testify that the statement you are making is correct?"

"Yes, a dozen if you like," said Travis, boldly. "Give me the book, and I'll come back this afternoon.

I didn't think there'd be such a fuss about getting out a little money."

"Wait a moment. Why don't your brother come himself?"

"Because he's sick. He's down with the measles," said Travis.

The cashier signaled to Dick to stand up.

"You will be glad to find that he has recovered," said the cashier.

With an exclamation of anger, Travis started for the door. But he was too late. He was facing a burly policeman, who seized him by the arm, saying, "Not so fast, my man. I want you."

"Let me go," exclaimed Travis, struggling to free himself.

"I'm afraid not," said the officer. "You'd better not make a fuss, or I may have to hurt you a little." Travis sullenly resigned himself to his fate, darting a look of rage at Dick.

"I believe this is yours," said the cashier, handing the bankbook to Dick. "Do you wish to draw out any money?"

"Two dollars," said Dick.

"Very well. Write an order for the amount."

Before doing so, Dick, looked at Travis and began to feel sorry for him.

"Won't you let him go?" Dick said to the policeman. "I've got my bankbook back, and I don't want anything done to him."

"Sorry," said the officer, "but I'm not allowed to do it. He'll have to stand trial."

"I'm sorry for you, Travis," said Dick. "I didn't want you arrested. I only wanted my bankbook back."

"Curse you!" said Travis, scowling with hatred. "Wait till I get free. See if I don't fix you."

"You needn't pity him too much," said the officer. "I know him now. He's been to the Island before."

"It's a lie," said Travis, violently.

"Don't be too noisy, my friend," said the officer. "If you've got no more business here, we'll be going."

He left with his prisoner, and Dick, having drawn his two dollars, left the bank.

"I'll keep my book a little safer hereafter," thought Dick. "Now I must go and see Tom Wilkins."

Returning to the City Hall Park, Dick soon caught up with Tom Wilkins.

"How are you, Tom?" he said. "How's your mother?"

"She's better, Dick, thank you. She felt worried about bein' turned out into the street. But I gave her that money from you, and now she feels a good deal easier."

"I've got some more for you, Tom," said Dick, producing two dollars from his pocket.

"I ought not to take it from you, Dick."

"Oh, it's all right, Tom. Don't be afraid."

"But you may need it yourself."

"There's plenty more where that came from."

"Any way, one dollar will be enough. With that we can pay the rent."

"You'll want the other to buy something to eat."

"You're very kind, Dick."

"I'd ought to be. I've only got myself to take care of."

"Well, I'll take it for my mother's sake. When

you want anything done just call on Tom Wilkins."

"All right. Next week, if your mother doesn't get better, I'll give you some more."

Tom thanked Dick gratefully. As Dick walked away, he felt good about being able to help Tom and his family. He remembered that, nine months earlier, Mr. Whitney had given Dick five dollars. And he remembered that Mr. Whitney had told him that he could repay it to some other boy who was struggling upward. Dick realized that he was only paying up an old debt.

When Fosdick came home in the evening, Dick told him what had happened at the bank.

"You're in luck," said Fosdick. "I guess we'd better not trust the bureau-drawer again."

"I mean to carry my book round with me," said Dick. "I must go down and tell her she not to expect Travis back. Poor fellow, I pity him."

CHAPTER 24

Dick Receives a Letter

It was about a week after Dick's recovery of his bankbook that Fosdick brought home a copy of the *Daily Sun*.

"Your name is in the newspaper, Dick," Fosdick said.

"It is?" said Dick, as he washed the shoe polish off his hands. "They haven't put me up for mayor, have they? If they have, I won't accept. It would interfere too much with my private business."

"No," said Fosdick, "they haven't put you up for office yet. But if you want to see your name in print, here it is."

After drying his hands, Dick took the paper. Fosdick pointed to a particular item on the page. It was a list of advertised letters—letters that did not have enough of an address for the post office to deliver them. There he saw the name "Ragged Dick."

"So it is," he said. "Do you suppose it means me?"

"I don't know of any other Ragged Dick—do you?"

"No," said Dick. "It must be me. But I don't know of anybody that would be likely to write to me."

"Perhaps it is Frank Whitney," suggested Fosdick. "Didn't he promise to write to you?"

"Yes," said Dick.

"Where is he now?"

"He was going to a boarding-school in Connecticut. The name of the town was Barnton."

"Very likely the letter is from him. You had better go to the post office tomorrow morning and ask for it."

"Maybe they won't give it to me."

"Suppose you wear the old clothes you used to a year ago, when Frank first saw you? They won't have any doubt of your being Ragged Dick then."

"I guess I will. I'll be sort of ashamed to be seen in 'em though," said Dick. "But it would be worth it to get a letter from Frank. I'd like to see him."

The next morning Dick dressed in the long disused clothes he had been wearing when he first met Frank. Looking at himself in the little mirror, Dick felt rather ashamed of his appearance.

He managed to slip out of the house into unobserved. After polishing the shoes of to two or three regular customers who came downtown early in the morning, he made his way down Nassau Street to the post office. Next to one of the windows was a sign that said "Advertised Letters."

Stepping up to the window, he said, "There's a letter for me. I saw it advertised in the *Sun* yesterday."

"What name?" asked the clerk.

"Ragged Dick."

"That's an odd name," said the clerk, looking at him with curiosity. "Are you Ragged Dick?"

"If you don't believe me, look at my clothes," said Dick.

"That's pretty good proof, certainly," said the clerk, laughing. "If that isn't your name, it deserves to be."

"I believe in dressin' up to your name," said Dick.

"Do you know any one in Barnton, Connecticut?" asked the clerk, who had by this time found the letter.

"Yes," said Dick. "I know a fellow that's at boarding school there."

"I think this must be yours, then."

The clerk handed the letter to Dick. He stepped away from the window, hastily opened the letter, and began to read.

Dear Dick,

"You must excuse my addressing this letter to "Ragged Dick," but, I don't know what your last name is or where you live. I am afraid there is not much chance of your getting this letter, but I hope you will.

I have thought of you very often, and wondered how you were getting along.

Barnton is a very pretty country town, only about six miles from Hartford. The boarding school is in a large two-story house. There are twenty students. We are taught by the head of the school, Mr. Munroe, and an assistant teacher.

There are about fifty acres of land belonging to Mr. Munroe, so we have plenty of room for play. About a quarter of a mile from the house there is a good-sized pond. In the summer we go swimming. In the winter there is splendid skating on the pond. Besides this, we play ball a good deal. So we have a pretty good time, although we study pretty hard too. I am getting on very well in my studies.

I wish you were here, Dick. I think you would like it.

I have to hand in a composition tomorrow on the life and character of George Washington. I don't much like writing compositions. I would rather write letters.

If you get this letter, you must be sure to answer it as soon as possible. I don't mind if your writing does look like "hens' tracks," as you told me once.

Goodbye, Dick.

Your friend,

Frank Whitney

Dick read the letter with much satisfaction. He felt a new sense of importance in having a letter addressed to him. It was the first letter he had ever received. And thanks to Fosdick, he could not only read writing, but he could write a very good hand himself.

"He's a good friend," thought Dick. "I wish I could see him again. He'd find me a little more respectable than when he first saw me."

Dick had by this time got up to Printing House Square. Standing on Spruce Street, near the *Tribune* office, was his old enemy, Micky Maguire.

Seeing Dick dressed neatly over the last nine months had irritated Micky. He didn't like the idea of Dick acting superior. Now his astonished eyes rested on Dick in his old clothing. It was a moment of triumph to him. He felt that "pride had had a fall."

"Them's nice clo'es you've got on," said he, sarcastically, as Dick came up.

"Yes," said Dick, promptly. "I've been employin' your tailor. If my face was only dirty we'd be taken for twin brothers."

"I don't b'lieve you've got any better clo'es anymore," said Micky.

"All right," said Dick. "I won't charge you nothin' for what you believe."

A customer arrived and wanted Micky to shine his shoes. Dick went back to his room to change his clothes before resuming business.

CHAPTER 25

Dick Writes His First Letter

When Fosdick reached home in the evening, Dick showed him the letter.

"It's a nice letter," said Fosdick, after reading it. "When are you going to answer it?"

"I don't know," said Dick, dubiously. "I never writ a letter."

"That's no reason why you shouldn't. There's always a first time, you know."

"I don't know what to say," said Dick.

"Get some paper and sit down to it, and you'll find enough to say. You can do that this evening instead of studying."

"If you'll look it over afterwards and shine it up a little."

"Yes, if it needs it; but I rather think Frank would like it best just as you wrote it."

After various preparations, Dick at last got settled down to his task and, before the evening was over, a letter was written.

Dear Frank,

I got your letter this morning and was very glad to hear you hadn't forgotten Ragged Dick. I ain't so ragged as I was.

I've give up sleepin' in boxes and old wagons. It didn't agree with my constitution. I've hired a room in Mott Street and have got a private tuter, who rooms with me and looks after my studies in the evenin'. Mott Street ain't very fashionable, but my mansion on Fifth Avenue isn't finished yet.

I haven't forgot what you and your uncle said to me, and I'm tryin' to grow up respectable. I haven't been to Tony Pastor's or the Old Bowery for ever so long. I'd rather save up my money to support me in my old age.

I've got so as to read pretty well, so my tutor says. I've been studyin' geography and grammar also.

You must have a good time at school with the swimmin' and skatin'.

When are you comin' to the city? I wish you'd write and let me know when you do, and I'll call and see you. I'll leave my business in the hands of my numerous clerks and go round with you. There's lots of things you didn't see when you was here before. They're getting on fast at Central Park. It looks better than it did a year ago.

I hope you'll write to me again soon. Goodbye, Frank. Thank you for all your

kindness. Direct your next letter to No. __,
Mott Street.

Your friend,
Dick Hunter

When Dick had written the last word, he
leaned back in his chair and looked over the letter with much satisfaction.

"I didn't think I could have wrote such a
long letter, Fosdick," he said. "I guess there's
plenty of mistakes in it. Just look at it, and see."

Fosdick took the letter and read it over carefully.

"Yes, there are some mistakes," he said. "But
it sounds so much like you that I think it would
be better to let it go just as it is."

"Is it good enough to send?" asked Dick,
anxiously.

"Yes; it seems to me to be quite a good letter. It is written just as you talk. Nobody but you
could have written such a letter, Dick."

The next day, Dick took the letter down to
the post office and mailed it. As he was coming
out of the building, he met Johnny Nolan on the
steps.

"What are you doin' down here, Dick?"
asked Johnny.

"I've been mailin' a letter."

"Who sent you?"

"Nobody."

"I mean, who writ the letter?"

"I wrote it myself."

"Can you write letters?" asked Johnny, in amazement.

"Why shouldn't I?"

"I didn't know you could write. I can't."

"Then you ought to learn."

"I went to school once; but it was too hard work, so I give it up."

"How'd you ever expect to know anything if you don't try?"

"I can't learn."

"You can if you want to."

Johnny Nolan was evidently of a different opinion. He was a good-natured boy, but utterly lacking in energy and ambition. Johnny was not at all like Dick.

CHAPTER 26

An Exciting Adventure

Dick now began to look about for a position in a store or an office. He spent half of each day blacking boots and the rest of the time looking for another job. He found that he could earn enough in half a day to pay all his necessary expenses, including the room rent. Fosdick wanted to pay his half, but Dick refused, insisting it was compensation for Henry's services as instructor.

Unfortunately, business was very slow, and merchants, instead of hiring new assistants, were more interested in getting rid of the ones they already had. After making several applications, Dick began to think he would have to stick to his profession until the next season.

One Wednesday afternoon Henry Fosdick was sent by his employer on an errand to Brooklyn. Dick decided to accompany him. The two boys walked down to the South Ferry, and, paying their two cents each, boarded the ferryboat.

They remained at the stern and stood by the

railing, watching the great city receding from view. Beside them was a gentleman with two children, a girl of eight and a little boy of six. The children were talking energetically to their father. While he was pointing out some object of interest to the little girl, the boy crept unobserved beneath the guardrail. Stepping incautiously to the edge of the boat, he fell over into the foaming water.

At the child's scream, the father looked up. With a cry of horror, he sprang to the edge of the boat. He would have plunged in, but, being unable to swim, would have been no help to the boy.

"My child!" he exclaimed in anguish. "Who will save my little Johnny? I'll give anything to if someone will just save him!"

There were only a few passengers on board at the time, and nearly all these were either in the cabin or standing forward.

It happened that Dick was an expert swimmer. He no sooner saw the boy fall than he resolved to rescue him, even before he heard the father's anguished cries.

Little Johnny had already risen once and gone under for the second time when Dick plunged in. He reached the child none too soon. Just as he was sinking for the third and last time, Dick caught him by the jacket. Dick was strong, but Johnny clung to him so tightly that the bootblack had difficulty keeping them both afloat.

"Put your arms round my neck," said Dick.

The little boy mechanically obeyed and clung

with a grasp strengthened by his terror. In this position Dick could bear his weight better. But the ferryboat was receding fast. It was impossible to reach it. The father, his face pale with terror, saw the brave boy's struggles and prayed with agonizing fervor that he would be successful. They were, however, a long distance from either shore. It was not likely that Dick would be able to swim to safety with the child clinging to him.

Fortunately, two men in a rowboat were nearby. They had seen the accident and quickly rowed toward the desperate pair.

"Keep up a little longer," they shouted, bending to their oars. "We are coming."

Dick heard the shout, and it put fresh strength into him. He battled manfully in the treacherous water, his eyes fixed on the approaching boat.

"Hold on tight, little boy," he said. "There's a boat coming."

The little boy did not see the boat. His eyes were closed to shut out the fearful sight of the water. Six long, steady strokes, and the boat dashed along side. Strong hands seized Dick and his youthful burden and drew them into the boat, both dripping with water.

"Thank God!" exclaimed the father, as he saw the child's rescue. "That brave boy will be rewarded."

"You've had a pretty narrow escape, young chap," said one of the boatmen to Dick. "It was a pretty tough job you undertook."

"Yes," said Dick. "That's what I thought when

I was in the water. If it hadn't been for you, I don't know what would have happened to us."

The father was waiting on the wharf to when the rowboat arrived with his little boy and Dick. He shed tears of joy as he took the child in his arms. Dick was about to withdraw modestly, but the gentleman caught sight of him. Putting down the child, he approached Dick and clasped his hand with emotion.

"My brave boy, I owe you a debt I can never repay. If it weren't for you, my precious little boy would have been lost to me forever."

"It wasn't any trouble," he said, modestly. "I'm a good swimmer."

"Not many boys would have risked their lives for a stranger," said the gentleman. "But," he added with a sudden thought, as his glance rested on Dick's dripping clothes, "both you and my little boy will catch cold in those clothes. I have a friend who lives close by. We will go to his house so you can dry off."

Dick protested that he never caught colds. But Fosdick, who had now joined them, urged Dick to accept the offer. The gentleman hailed a cab. A few moments later the carriage stopped in front of a pleasant house on a side street. Soon Dick found himself in a warm bed.

"I ain't used to goin' to bed quite so early," thought Dick. "This is the strangest excursion I ever took."

In about an hour the door of his room opened, and a servant appeared, carrying a handsome new suit of clothes.

"You are to put these on," said the servant. "But you needn't get up till you feel like it."

"Whose clothes are they?" asked Dick.

"They are yours."

"Mine! Where did they come from?"

"Mr. Rockwell sent out and bought them for you. They are the same size as your wet ones."

"Is he here now?"

"No. He bought another suit for the little boy and has gone back to New York. Here's a note he asked me to give you."

Dick opened the note.

> Please accept these clothes as the first installment of a debt that I can never repay. I have asked to have your wet suit dried, when you can reclaim it. Please call on me tomorrow at my office, No. ___, Pearl Street.
>
> Your friend,
> James Rockwell

CHAPTER 27

Conclusion

The new suit fitted Dick as well as if it had been made expressly for him.

"He's done the handsome thing," said Dick to himself. "But there wasn't no cause for his giving me these clothes. My lucky stars are shinin' pretty bright now. Jumpin' into the water pays better than shinin' boots, but I don't think I'd like to try it more than once a week."

About eleven o'clock the next morning Dick went to the address on Pearl Street that Mr. Rockwell had given him. The building was a large and handsome warehouse. He entered and found Mr. Rockwell sitting at a desk. As soon as Mr. Rockwell saw Dick, he got up and shook his hand.

"My young friend," he said, "you have done me so great service that I wish to be of some service to you in return. Tell me about yourself, and what plans or wishes you have formed for the future."

Dick related his past history and told Mr. Rockwell of his desire to get into a store or an office and of the failure of all his applications thus far. The merchant listened attentively. When Dick had finished, Mr. Rockwell handed him a piece of paper and a pen said, "Will you write your name on this piece of paper?"

Dick wrote in a free, bold hand the name Richard Hunter. Mr. Rockwell surveyed it approvingly.

"How would you like to work in my office as a clerk, Richard?" he asked.

Dick was about to say "Bully," but he caught himself and answered, "Very much."

"I suppose you know something of arithmetic, do you not?"

"Yes, sir."

"Then you may consider yourself hired at a salary of ten dollars a week. You may come next Monday morning."

"Ten dollars!" repeated Dick, thinking he must have misunderstood.

"Yes. Will that be sufficient?"

"It's more than I can earn," said Dick, honestly.

"Perhaps it is at first," said Mr. Rockwell, smiling; "but I am willing to pay you that. And I will advance you as fast as your progress will justify it."

Dick was so excited that he could hardly speak. But he managed to say, "I'll try to serve you so faithfully, sir, that you won't regret having hired me."

"And I think you will succeed," said Mr. Rockwell, encouragingly. "I will not detain you any longer, for I have some important business to attend to. I shall expect to see you on Monday morning."

Dick left the office so overjoyed that he hardly knew whether he was standing on his head or his heels. Ten dollars a week was to him a fortune. Indeed he would have been glad, only the day before, to get a place at three dollars a week. He reflected that with the stock of clothes which he had now on hand, he could save up at least half of it, and even then live better than he was used to. And savings account, instead of being diminished, would be steadily increasing. Then he was to be advanced if he deserved it. It was a bright prospect for a boy who, only a year before, could neither read nor write, and depended for a night's lodging upon the chance hospitality of an alleyway or old wagon.

"I wish Fosdick was as well off as I am," he thought generously. But he determined to help his less fortunate friend and assist him up the ladder as he advanced himself.

When Dick entered his room on Mott Street, he discovered that someone else had been there before him, and two articles of clothing had disappeared.

"By gracious!" he exclaimed. "Somebody's stole my Washington coat and pants. Maybe it's an agent of Barnum's, who expects to make a fortun' by exhibitin' the valuable wardrobe of a gentleman of fashion."

A few days later he saw Micky Maguire wearing the missing clothes. He never found out if Micky had stolen them himself. But he felt that it was fitting to be rid of the old clothes, now that he was on his way to a new life.

Although it was yet only noon, Dick did not go out again with his brush and polish. He felt that it was time to retire from that business. He would leave his clients to other boys less fortunate than himself. That evening Dick and Fosdick had a long conversation. Fosdick was overjoyed at his friend's success. He also had good news: his pay had been advanced to six dollars a week.

"I think we can afford to leave Mott Street now," he continued. "This house isn't as neat as it might be, and I'd be happy to live in a nicer quarter of the city."

"All right," said Dick. "We'll hunt up a new room tomorrow. And maybe I'll try to get my regular customers to take Johnny Nolan in my place. That boy needs somebody to look out for him."

"You might give him your box and brush, too, Dick."

"No," said Dick. "I'll give him some new ones, but mine I want to keep, to remind me of the hard times I've had, when I was an ignorant bootblack and never expected to be anything better."

"When you were Ragged Dick. You must drop that name, and think of yourself now as—"

"Mr. Richard Hunter," said Dick, smiling.

"A young gentleman on the way to fame and fortune," added Fosdick.

AFTERWORD

About the Author

In 1896, poor health and failing eyesight forced Horatio Alger to retire from his career as a writer. He was sixty-four years old. Over the previous thirty years, he had written more than one hundred books. Like *Ragged Dick*, most of the books are stories of adolescent boys who succeed by overcoming difficult personal circumstances. In some respects, Alger's own life followed a similar pattern. The second half of his life was very different from the first half.

Horatio Alger was born in Chelsea, Massachusetts, in 1834. His father was a Unitarian minister who also taught school to help make ends meet. Alger developed asthma as a child. He was always small for his age. (Even as an adult, he was just over five feet tall.) In his first few years of school, he did not do well academically. This may have been in part the result of a stutter that made him embarrassed to speak up in class. When he was ten years old, his family moved to the town of Marlborough, Massachusetts, where he enrolled in the local prep school. His academic work improved enough that, at the age of sixteen, he was accepted to Harvard University. A relative helped pay his tuition. At Harvard he did well and won several awards and prizes. He later said that his four years at Harvard were the most enjoyable years of his life.

After graduating, he attempted to earn a living by writing. Some of his poems and stories were printed in popular magazines and newspapers, but he could not support himself through his writing. For a while, he worked as a teacher to supplement his income. He also spent several months traveling in Europe. In 1857 he entered Harvard Divinity School. When the Civil War broke out in 1861, his poor health and small size prevented him from joining the Union Army.

In 1864, he accepted the position of minister at the First Unitarian Church in Brewster, Massachusetts. His salary was eight hundred dollars a year and the work allowed him time to pursue his writing career. This apparently ideal situation lasted just over a year. In March of 1866, he was accused of having sexual relations with several teenage boys in his parish. He did not deny the charge. The congregation dismissed him with the understanding that he was to leave town.

Alger's dismissal from the church in Brewster proved to be a turning point in his life and in his career. There is no way to know for certain whether or not Alger continued his molestation of teenagers. However, there is evidence to suggest that he did not. Some of that evidence can be found in a poem he published a few years later entitled "Friar Anselmo's Sin." The poem begins: "Friar Anselmo (God's grace may he win)/ Committed one sad day a deadly sin." It then goes on to describe how the lonely and miserable monk helps a wounded traveler. An angel then appears to the monk and assures him he has done the right thing and that such good works can erase his sin: "Thy guilty stains shall be washed white again,/By noble service done thy fellow-men." If Alger was describing himself in this poem, it would suggest that he felt he must spend the rest of his life doing "noble service" for humankind in order to wash clean the stain of guilt from his child molestation. And, given the direction his life took after 1866, this seems to be what he attempted to do.

Less than a month after leaving Brewster, Alger was living in a rented room in New York City. In the mid-1860s, many ambitious people had been drawn to New York in the boom that followed the Civil War. The city seemed to offer boundless opportunities. Beneath that glittering surface, however, there were filthy slums and extreme poverty. In many neighborhoods, the streets were clogged with trash and garbage. Some neighborhoods, such as Five Points, were so dangerous that policemen were reluctant to walk there alone. There were more than 60,000 abandoned or neglected children roaming the streets of New York. This is the world that Alger entered. The homeless, abused children of New York City offered Alger the opportunity to do "noble service for [his] fellow-men."

One way Alger offered service was through his writing. In 1866, he wrote *Ragged Dick*. One of his aims was to make people aware of the plight of the homeless children of New York. He did this by showing how such boys lived and what their backgrounds were. Dick is on the street because he was left alone when his father disappeared at sea and his mother died. Johnny Nolan is on the street because he chose to leave home after his drunken and abusive father almost killed him with an iron skillet. Henry Fosdick is on the street because his father drowned and left him alone. Such boys live hand-to-mouth, eating when they can afford to and sleeping wherever they can. In addition to showing people what life was like for such children, Alger also showed how, with a little help, some boys (such as Dick and Fosdick) could turn their lives around and become productive members of society. Making people aware that such children existed was a first step toward getting people to help them.

A second way that Alger offered service was by becoming a philanthropist—a person who gives money and time to help others. Alger became friendly with Charles L. Brace, the founder of the Children's Aid Society. This organization was designed to take homeless or abused youths out of the city and place them in homes upstate or out West. The Society also established Newsboys' Lodging House where homeless boys could find food and shelter. Alger contributed much of his money to this and other such organizations. Alger also worked with businessmen to help find decent jobs for needy juveniles. He helped raise money for Five Points Mission, the YMCA, the Children's Aid Society, and the Newsboys' Lodging House. Most of the money that Alger earned from *Ragged Dick* and his other books, he spent on needy children.

Alger pushed for child welfare in his books and in his life. One specific example is his book *Phil the Fiddler* (1871). When Alger arrived in New York City, the "*padrone* system" was well established. In this system, *padrones* would promise rural Italians that they would take their children to New York and get them good jobs. When the children arrived from Europe, they were forced to live in overcrowded slum rooms and were sent out every day as beggars or street musicians. Everything they earned went to their *padrone*. In his novel *Phil the Fiddler*, Alger raised public consciousness of this cruel system of child slavery. Alger and others lobbied lawmakers. A year after the book was published, the New York State Legislature passed a law against cruelty to children and, in a short time, the *padrone* system ceased to exist.

By raising public consciousness of the terrible situation of homeless children and by contributing his time and money to the cause he believed in, Alger appears to have done his best to "wash white again" the stain of his own abuse of children during his year in Brewster.

Alger enjoyed his greatest popularity between 1867 and 1873. But he continued to write juvenile literature up until 1896. After 1873, he spent some of his time traveling to Europe and to the West, where he found ideas for new settings for his books. By 1896, his health was failing, so he left the city for good and moved in with his sister in Natick, Massachusetts. He died in 1899. Despite the strong sales of his books in the early years, he was not wealthy, having given away much of his money to homeless boys and charitable organizations that helped such children.

Like Ragged Dick, Horatio Alger turned his life around and made a success of himself. And, like Mr. Whitney, Mr. Greyson, and Mr. Rockwell, he showed compassion for children in need and a willingness to help them find a better life.

About the Book

In the first chapter of *Ragged Dick*, Dick is a self-indulgent bootblack who lives hand-to-mouth. He has one raggedy set of clothes. He sleeps in whatever wooden box happens to be available. Each day he spends all the money he earns and wakes up the next morning penniless. He can barely read and write and does not know much arithmetic.

By the last chapter of the novel, Dick has a bank account with over one hundred dollars in it. He is about to start a job in an office at the impressive salary of ten dollars a week. He has two good suits of clothes. He lives in a rented room and is planning to move to a better room. He can read and write. He knows some arithmetic.

Dick's changing name reflects his improving situation over the course of the novel. He starts out as Ragged Dick. He becomes Dick Hunter when he opens a bank account. And he becomes Richard Hunter when he writes his name for Mr. Rockwell.

There are two elements in the novel that account for Dick's change. One of those elements is luck. At two critical moments in his life, Dick happens to be in the right place at the right time. The first of these is when, in Chapter 3, Dick happens to be nearby as Mr. Whitney tells his nephew Frank that he cannot show him around the city. Dick offers to show Frank the sights. This leads to his getting a suit of clothes, a gift of five dollars, and—even more important—a good friend. But most important of all, the event gives Dick a glimpse into what his life could be. As soon as Dick puts on Frank's clothes, the hotel clerk who tried to stop him from entering the hotel a few minutes earlier lets him pass without saying a word.

At the end of Chapter 8, Frank suggests that Dick could go to night school to become better educated. Dick replies, "... since I've got to talkin' with you, I think more about [going to school]. I guess I'll begin to go." Frank helps Dick see what he is lacking and inspires him to improve himself.

". . . in order to succeed well, you must manage to get as good an education as you can. Until you do, you cannot get a position in an office, even to run errands."

"That's so," said Dick. "I never thought how awful ignorant I was till now."

"That can be fixed with hard work," said Frank. "A year will do a great deal for you.'"

"I'll see what I can do," said Dick, energetically.

Dick's chance encounter with Frank and Mr. Whitney is the first step in his deciding to improve himself. He becomes conscious of the possibility of changing his life.

The second time luck plays an important role in Dick's life is in the next-to-last chapter of the book.

Dick happens to be on the ferry when James Rockwell's son falls overboard. "He no sooner saw the boy fall than he resolved to rescue him. . . ." This event changes his life by leading him to a good job and the real possibility of becoming "respectable."

In each case, the lucky coincidence of being in the right place at the right time leads to significant changes in Dick's life. But just being there is not enough. When Dick overhears Frank and Mr. Whitney, he recognizes the possibility of the situation: "Being an enterprising young man, he saw an opportunity and decided to take advantage of it." When he sees Johnny Rockwell fall overboard, he reacts automatically. In both cases, if Dick had not acted either consciously or automatically, the events would not have affected his life as they did. What makes the difference is how Dick reacts to the situations. In other words, the sort of person Dick is makes the difference. This, then, is the second element that determines Dick's success—his character.

Alger makes it clear that Dick is not perfect. When we first meet him, he spends every cent he earns on entertainment, gambling, and treating other boys to oyster stew. At the beginning of the first chapter, he has spent all his money going to the show at the Old Bowery Theater. He will not have money for breakfast until he has earned it. And he sometimes plays unkind tricks on people, such as giving them wrong directions.

But he also has many good characteristics. He is hardworking. In the first chapter, he is sorry that he overslept, saying that he should have "been up an hour ago" so as not to miss customers. He works hard to get customers. "Dick's business hours had commenced.... His shoeshine box was ready for use, and he looked sharply in the faces of all who passed, asking each, 'Shine yer boots, sir?'" He is "always on the look-out for business."

He is honest. When he is asked if he ever steals, he replies, "No, and I wouldn't. Lots of boys does it, but I wouldn't." He soon proves his honesty by his action of returning Mr. Greyson's change, to the man's surprise.

He is generous and he cares about others. When he sees Johnny Nolan "looking hungrily into the restaurant," Dick treats him to breakfast. When Fosdick wants to pay part of the rent for their room, Dick will not let him. When Fosdick needs a new suit, Dick helps pay for it.

He is clever. As he shows Frank around New York, he explains to his new friend that the "Grand Closing-out Sale" is a scam. He shows Frank how the lost-wallet scam works. He tricks a swindler into returning the fifty dollars he took from a country boy. Once Fosdick becomes his tutor, Dick learns to read and write quickly.

One of the most important qualities is his ability to see long-term goals and to keep working toward them. After telling Frank he is thinking about becoming more educated, he actually follows through. Shortly after Frank leaves, Dick opens a savings account. "That way, he would have some money to fall back on in case of an emergency. He had been used to living day-to-day without a penny ahead. But now a vision of respectability floated before his mind." He recognizes the truth of Mr. Whitney's words: ". . . your future position depends mainly upon yourself, and that it will be high or low as you choose to make it."

It is all of these personal qualities—hard work, honesty, generosity, concern for others, cleverness, and a vision of the future—that enable Dick to make the most of the luck that comes his way.

A particularly important lesson that Dick learns from his chance meeting with Frank and his uncle is to pass along one's gifts to others. When Mr. Whitney offers Dick five dollars, Dick says he has not earned that money. Mr. Whitney replies, "I give it to you because I remember my own friendless youth. I hope it may be useful to you. Sometime when you are a prosperous man, you can repay it by helping to some poor boy who is struggling upward as you are now." And Dick does remember this lesson. He helps Tom Wilkins and his family by giving Tom five dollars to pay the rent and buy some food.

As Dick walked away, he felt good about being able to help Tom and his family. He remembered that, nine months earlier, Mr. Whitney had given Dick five dollars. And he remembered that Mr. Whitney had told him that he could repay it to some other boy who was struggling upward. Dick realized that he was only paying up an old debt.

Alger emphasizes the importance of Dick's personal qualities by presenting other characters to compare him with. Micky Maguire is the complete opposite of Dick. He is mean and a bully. He throws stones at people and picks fights for no reason. It seems unlikely that Micky will ever find the same sort of success that Dick finds. The fact that he appears in the final chapter wearing Dick's old clothes emphasizes this point. Unlike Dick's new clothes, Micky's "new" clothes are no better than his old ones were. He has not advanced and he probably never will.

Johnny Nolan is not mean but he is lazy. Alger creates Johnny's laziness to contrast with Dick's willingness to work hard. Clearly, Johnny will never find the success that Dick finds. Dick decides he will try to help Johnny out by giving him his old customers. Unlike Dick, Johnny "needs somebody to look out for him."

Henry Fosdick, on the other hand, is much more like Dick. He has the personal qualities that help him succeed. And he, too, knows how to take advantage of a lucky event. Mr. Greyson happens to enter the hat shop when Henry is applying for a job. And he enters just at the moment when Henry needs a reference. Henry seizes the opportunity by asking Mr. Greyson to recommend him. Because of Mr. Greyson's positive comments, Henry gets the job.

The lives of both Dick and Henry improve in part because of luck. But luck alone is not enough. One must have the positive personal qualities needed to make the most of one's opportunities. And one must be able to imagine a better future in order to take full advantage of the luck that comes one's way.